THE BRIDE'S BETRAYAL

DEBRA WEBB

Harlequin

INTRIGUE

Harlequin® INTRIGUE™

ISBN-13: 978-1-335-69074-6

The Bride's Betrayal

Copyright © 2026 by Debra Webb

Recycling programs for this product may not exist in your area.

Harlequin Enterprises ULC
22 Adelaide St. West, 41st Floor
Toronto, Ontario M5H 4E3, Canada
www.Harlequin.com

HarperCollins Publishers
Macken House, 39/40 Mayor Street Upper,
Dublin 1, D01 C9W8, Ireland
www.HarperCollins.com

Printed in Lithuania

1 2 3 4 5 6 7 8 9 10 LIT 28 27 26 25

"I just spent nearly two years in prison.

"I am very well aware of what it feels like to be stifled."

Chance smiled.

He had the nicest smile.

Rory banished the thought that popped into her head every single time the man's lips turned up. She had to stop looking at him that way. This was a business relationship. Her future depended on how this turned out.

As desperately as she needed a hero like him, he wasn't here to comfort her...only to help her find the truth and to support her efforts to prove her innocence.

Reader Note

Wow! Writing Rory's story was a rollercoaster ride! I hope you'll love this newest Colby Agency story. What is a woman to do when no one believes the truth? Find out by following along on Rory's journey. By the way, this story is set in my hometown of Scottsboro, Alabama. Please remember that I respect all those who serve in law enforcement but sometimes there's a bad apple depicted in my stories. And sometimes, it's only an illusion. See if you can figure out who's telling the truth.

CAST OF CHARACTERS

Aurora "Rory" Harris—Her husband was brutally murdered on their wedding night and Rory has spent two years in prison for his murder—can she prove she's innocent?

Chance Rader—The Colby Agency has sent him to help Rory find the truth, but will either one of them survive?

Detective Raymond Fowler—He put Rory away once. He isn't about to allow her to get this second chance of getting away with murder.

Anthony and Eudora Harris—Rory murdered their son, Pete. The couple would do anything to keep Rory in prison.

Austin Wilkins—Rory's brother, her only family. But can he help her save herself?

Deputy Shane Carters—He has a secret...they all have secrets. Will he protect Rory from the truth?

Victoria Colby-Camp and Jamie Colby—Victoria, with the help of her granddaughter Jamie, will ensure the Colby legacy goes on for another generation.

Chapter One

Monday, June 15

Kindred Residence
Tupelo Pike
Scottsboro, Alabama, 2:00 p.m.

Rory Harris stood very still for a long time after getting out of her brother's car.

It was a warm day. The sun was shining, and she was home for the first time in almost two years.

Two years.

Two long years. First in the Jackson County jail, and then in the Julia Tutwiler Prison for Women…for a murder she did not commit.

A collage of emotions whirled inside her like a tornado building in intensity, making her heart pound and her skin feel too cold. All those hours…the days and weeks of cowering in fear of the other inmates. All that time wondering if she would survive the next minute, much less the next day. Over a hundred weeks of her life…lost to fear and uncertainty.

But now she was home. She was free. This was a huge

deal. An opportunity to right a grave wrong. She should be happy.

Somehow the reality hadn't sunk in…maybe by tomorrow.

"Well, damn, Rory."

Rory glanced over the top of the car, where her brother, Austin Wilkins, stood on the driver's side. She followed his gaze toward the little white house that had belonged to their aunt. On the front porch, the old wooden screen door stood open. Not unusual. The thing never had stayed closed properly unless it was latched. But it was the front door behind the rickety screen door that held her brother's attention. The pale pink wooden slab had words spray-painted in black on it.

You Should Die Too

Austin swore again and stamped off toward the house their aunt had left Rory. Lulu had been their favorite aunt—their only living relative. That she had died while Rory was in prison was just another travesty in the horror movie that was her life. She suddenly felt sick. Sick of trying to prove her innocence. Sick of being looked at like she was a monster.

Sick of it all.

But there was nothing she could do except keep going and hoping the truth would come out. That might be the biggest travesty of all—the helplessness.

With nothing else to do, she trudged after her brother. She had begged him to forget about her. To pretend she no longer existed. To stay away. Get on with his life.

But he refused. She was all he had, he insisted.

It was true. Only the two of them were left. They had clung together since they were kids and their parents died in a house fire. Lulu had raised them. She'd had a heck of a time getting custody in the beginning. She was forty-nine with a less than sterling reputation around the little town of Scottsboro, and there had been some back-and-forth during the hearings. Finally, the judge, a reasonable man with a broader view of things, had come to the conclusion that for all her eccentricities, Lulu was a good person who loved Rory and Austin, and that was more important than social status and her standing in a church.

"If I find out who did this," Austin threatened as Rory reached the porch.

She put a hand on his arm. "Please don't say or do anything to anyone. The more we fight back, the worse it will get."

He nodded, his head hung in defeat. "I'll go out to the shed and see if I can find some of that paint." Before walking away, he thrust the key at her. "Go on in. Get settled. See if I did things right."

She smiled, accepted the key. "You always do everything right."

"So you say," he muttered as he bounded down the steps.

Rory turned to the door, ignored the ugly painted words. Lulu would be furious that anyone had dared to deface her precious pink door. She had been a total pink fanatic. She had painted the door on her house a lovely pink well before anyone else would have been so bold. Lulu always did things before anyone else had the courage. Just another characteristic that caused folks to give her the side-eye.

Deep breath. Rory walked inside. Felt an instant relief. *Home.* She and Austin had lived in this house from the time Rory was five and he was three. And it looked basically the same, even more than twenty years later.

Lulu had been an aging hippie who believed flowers, peace symbols, boho style and vibrant colors could solve most anything. Having a bit of medicinal marijuana also helped greatly, in Lulu's opinion. Though she had hidden her little therapeutic secret well, Rory had known. Her mother, Lulu's younger sister, often said that her big sister was a little crazy—but in a good way. Not that Rory could remember a whole lot about things her mom said, but Lulu had gone to great lengths to ensure they remembered as much as possible about their parents. She had made it as important a mission as sending them to school—maybe slightly more. As for church, they had regularly attended the Church of Lulu.

Rory smiled, the warmth her aunt had always prompted spreading through her now. There had been no one else in the world like her. The life-crushing events of two years ago had hurt Lulu almost as much as they had Rory.

The house smelled and looked clean. Austin had really gone above and beyond to ensure all was neat and tidy. There wasn't even a layer of dust on the furniture, no matter that no one had lived here in nearly a year. Rory picked up the framed photo of her and Austin and their parents. It was taken only weeks before their parents' deaths and the one photo left of the four of them together.

She moved around the room and studied the many photos her aunt had carefully curated. Lots of framed photos on the walls. Lots of her aunt's artwork as well. Lulu, actually Tallulah—Tallulah Kindred—had been an amazing artist. Not watercolors or oil paints. Graphite was her chosen medium, sometimes in shades of gray and black. Others were drawn using colored pencils. Somewhere in the house were stacks of drawing pads filled with her work. Rory vividly remembered sitting with her on First

Mondays on the downtown square and in the park on Art Sunday each fall while she drew portraits of anyone interested. Her ability had fascinated Rory.

Rory moved into the kitchen. She could really use a glass of water. She felt as if she'd walked miles and miles through the desert. Prison was like the desert in many ways. There was nothing familiar to someone who had never been there before…nothing to help you find your way or to survive. There was all manner of danger from things you didn't see coming or understand. It was crowded and at the same time desolate. Structured and at the same time chaotic. And sad, with no hope in sight. The cries and moaning at night had been the worst.

Rory shook off the memories. She was home now… for what it was worth.

Focus, Rory. Be thankful for whatever time you have.

Austin had ensured the kitchen was ready as well. She checked the fridge and a few of the cabinets, then smiled. Milk, butter and cheese—even yogurt, and her brother hated yogurt, but he knew Rory liked it. Canned and dry goods. Her most beloved cereal. She and Lulu had always eaten Lucky Charms but rarely at breakfast—it was their late-night snack. He'd even stocked up on her favorite soft drinks and chips.

She walked to the back door and stared out the window. The lawn was freshly mown. Lulu's flowers were blooming everywhere. Rory would be picking a bouquet for the table. The timeworn swing set still stood under that big old tree. Its frame rusty, the seats tattered. Rory's chest hurt with the memories of playing in this yard. Chasing her brother. Laughing. Even after losing their parents, the two of them had somehow found a way to be happy. To cling to Lulu as their buoy. No matter how tough times were financially more often than not, she and Austin were lucky they had someone who loved them so much.

Before moving away from the door, she noticed the new dead bolt. She wondered if there had been a break-in. She would have to remember to ask Austin about the addition.

Then she wandered to the other end of the little house and the tiny bedrooms. Lulu's was the largest and every bit as vibrant as she was. Rory's was at the end of the hall. Since Austin was so little when they moved here, he'd had the one nearest Lulu. Rory stalled at his door. His things, furniture and all, were gone now. Instead, there was a desk with a laptop and a bookcase loaded with books.

"I thought you needed an office more than you needed a third bedroom."

She glanced over her shoulder at her brother. She hadn't heard him come in. "Thank you, but I wish you hadn't gone to so much trouble."

"It was no trouble, really." He smiled. "The paint on the door is taken care of." He pulled his cell from his pocket and checked the time. "Jamie Colby should be calling you in about ten minutes."

Rory frowned. "Is the house phone still on?" Lulu had hated cell phones and any other device that connected a person to any sort of big network. Along with her wild child persona had come just a touch of paranoia. She had kept her old-fashioned landline forever. She had outright refused to have cable TV installed. Only the antenna and a single old-fashioned radio were allowed to deliver any sort of waves into her home, she'd insisted. No internet either.

"It is," Austin told her, "but there's a new cell phone for you in your room, and the internet is up and running."

This was amazing. "Oh my God, you really did far too much."

"The police never returned your laptop, and your phone was stolen," he argued. "It was the least I could do."

Rory went into the bedroom she had used until she moved in with Pete. Being with him was the happiest time of her life. She stood at the dresser her aunt had painted a turquoise just for her when Rory was fifteen. A framed photo of Rory and her brand-new husband on their wedding day had been placed there. Her heart swelled with emotion. How on earth had Austin gotten that photograph?

"When I picked up your stuff from the storage unit where Pete's folks had put it," Austin explained, "this was the only photo of the two of you they'd left. I think maybe it was an oversight since all the rest were gone. Anyway, I thought you might like having it framed and placed where you could see it."

She stared at her little brother then. His hair was not as dark as hers, his eyes a more common shade of blue. Even his complexion was a more medium color, not so pale like hers. And yet he'd always been like her twin in every other way. Sticking to her like glue as a little kid. Defending her adamantly as a teenager. And now, taking care of her when she had no one else.

She loved him to pieces.

She hugged him hard, then drew back so they could breathe. Emotion had crowded so tightly into her throat she couldn't speak for a moment. "Thank you. I really appreciate everything."

She picked up the frame and studied the photo. Pete's smile tugged at her senses. She missed him so much. How had their seemingly perfect life gone so very wrong on their wedding night? They had been so happy together. More bewildering, who would have wanted to hurt them?

Pete had been the nicest person anyone would ever hope to meet. He had never harmed anyone. And yet he was dead…murdered.

She forced the haunting thoughts away and focused on the happy moments of their wedding. The dress she had picked out had been the one of her dreams. A beautiful princess ball gown style. Of course it was far too expensive—way, way out of her price range. It didn't seem reasonable to pay such a price for a dress she would only wear once. But Lulu had insisted it wasn't a problem. A few weeks later, her aunt had called her to this little house to show off the dress. It was the most beautiful thing Rory had ever seen. But what made it truly perfect was that Lulu had made the dress exactly like the one Rory couldn't afford.

She set the photo back on the dresser. Pushed a smile into place for her brother. "You are the very best brother any sister could ever want."

Austin pointed to the phone lying next to the photo. "It's fully charged and ready to go." He gestured to the closet on the other side of the little room. "I hung up all your clothes—at least the ones they had put in boxes and left at the storage unit. If there were other things…" He shrugged. "I brought everything here that was in that unit. If anything is missing, I can ask them—"

"No." She got it. If there was anything else, Pete's parents would have likely thrown it away or burned it. Besides, she wasn't allowed to go near them or their home or the one she and Pete had shared. "I'm certain what you brought home is fine."

"If you're sure," he allowed.

"I'm sure."

Rory closed her eyes for a long moment and blocked

the images and sounds that tried to invade her head. She had worked hard to keep those memories at bay. Once the trial was over, what was the point of attempting to remember the details of that awful night or allowing the good memories from before that to torture her? Pete was gone. She had been charged with his murder and sentenced to decades in prison.

She was only standing here now because someone had made a mistake in the handling of evidence, and her lawyer had finally figured it out and managed to win a motion for retrial.

"Jamie's call will be on Zoom," Austin explained, dragging her back to the moment. "Let me walk you through the internet security stuff."

She nodded, ready to get out of this room—away from the photo that reminded her of all she had lost. In the office he had created, he showed her the login information and prepared the laptop for receiving the incoming call.

"You're ready," he said. "So you know, I added new dead bolts to both doors just in case. You'll find keys for those on that keychain I gave you. I charged the battery in Lulu's car. Got the oil changed, tires checked and filled the gas tank, so you have wheels."

"All of this is a tremendous help, Austin." All of it was overwhelming. She struggled to hold back the tears.

He waved her off. "It was nothing."

She knew that her brother was taking a couple of summer classes in addition to working full-time. This had to have been a big chunk out of his income, and she had no way to pay him back just now.

"I am going to pay you back," she argued. "Eventually."

"No way." He shook his head emphatically. "You took

care of me in a million ways growing up. This is the least I could do for you now."

Rather than argue further with him, she said, "You should head back to Nashville." She didn't want him driving back at night. It was silly, but she was old-fashioned that way. Her aunt had drilled a lot of old-fashioned ideas into their heads.

"I thought I would stay with you for a few days," he argued. "You shouldn't be alone."

Rory grabbed her brother and hugged him again. "I love you. I don't know what I would do without you."

He hugged her just as tightly. "We will fix this," he promised. "We have the opportunity now."

Rory drew back and smiled. "I know."

She said this just for him, because the truth was, there was no fixing this. No matter that she had this unexpected opportunity. Still, she would take it and the time out of that prison. But she didn't dare get her hopes up about staying out of that place.

"As much as I appreciate the offer, you need to go," she said firmly. "This is my battle, my tragedy. I am so thankful for your support, but I do not want it to become your battle again. You've done more than enough. The rest is up to me. Do you understand?"

He held her gaze a moment, his shining with the emotions tugging at him. "I do, but I still want to be here for you."

"You can be here *for* me," she said, "without being *here*. Okay?"

He exhaled a big breath. "If you're sure."

"I am. Now get back to your life. You're only a phone call away."

He smiled and nodded. "All right."

When he'd driven away, she closed and locked the door, the dead bolt as well. She wandered back into the kitchen for the water she'd forgotten. The chilled bottles of water in the fridge made her smile. He really had thought of everything. Then she went to the desk in Austin's old room and sat down to wait for the call from Jamie Colby.

She was home…even if only for a little while.

Even though she was expecting the sound, she jumped when the alert for the incoming call echoed in the room.

She squared her shoulders and accepted it. "Hello, this is Aurora Harris."

The blue-eyed, blond-haired woman who had visited her in prison smiled. "Rory, it's so good to see you at home."

Rory swallowed to wet her dry throat. "Thank you. It's good to be home." She decided not to mention the awful message that had been waiting for her on the door.

"Chance Rader is en route to your location as we speak. He landed in Huntsville a few minutes ago. He should be there in the next hour and a half or so."

Rory nodded. "I look forward to meeting him in person." They had spoken by phone when Jamie visited her at the prison. He had been finishing up an assignment and couldn't come that day.

"He is one of our very best investigators," Jamie assured her again. "As I explained to you before, everyone here at the agency will do all possible to help as well. Our research department is at Rader's disposal as are all our resources. You will have the very best working to find the facts."

"I appreciate your help more than you can imagine."

One big fact was that she could never in a dozen lifetimes have afforded to hire the Colby Agency—one of the top private investigation firms in the country…maybe the world. But Austin attended college with Jamie's younger brother, Luke. They were friends, and when Austin had dared to share her story with his new friend, Luke had jumped into action.

Rory had urged Austin not to tell people she was his sister, and to avoid talk of her and the case at all costs. He refused. Who could have imagined that her brother was telling the story to the one person in the world who might actually be able to help? The Colby Agency had insisted on taking her case pro bono.

"We are grateful to have the opportunity to right such an egregious wrong," Jamie went on. "As I told you before, I have reviewed your case thoroughly, and the holes in the investigation are easily seen in my opinion. The investigative and legal work was not up to standard, and your rights were trampled repeatedly because of that. We will see that it's done properly this time."

"Thank you."

But that, for Rory, was the downside to all this. No matter that the verdict had been overturned due to a single piece of evidence the DA's office failed to present, much less share. The nightmare was far from over. A new trial would happen, and the detective had been told to go back out and to do the job right this time if they wanted to go after Rory again. And they did. Oh, how they did. The Harris family, her dead husband's parents, were the wealthiest in the state—maybe in the whole Southeast. They were never going to stop until the person they believed had murdered their son was put away forever.

Even the thought of what they believed she had done hurt her to the core of her being. How could anyone believe such a thing?

"You hang in there," Jamie encouraged her. "We will get this done."

The call ended, and Rory closed the laptop. She picked up the cell phone her brother had bought for her. It was a lighter version of the turquoise color she liked so much. She was so grateful for all he'd done, but she worried about him. She didn't want this nightmare to follow him the rest of his life too.

Somehow, if this went the wrong way, she needed to convince him to forget about her and to move on with his life without her in it. He would resist, but it was the best course of action if this didn't work out. As much confidence as she had in the Colby Agency based on all she had read about them, this was not exactly a simple situation. The Harris family would not let this go without a long and ruthless fight.

She went back to her bedroom and picked up the photo of her and Pete. Her heart hurt. She had loved him so much. So, so much. They had dated for only two months before deciding to move in together. Then, four months later, they got married, and her world was turned upside down. Her wonderful life had been destroyed completely. Nothing had survived that night.

She had loved her life. Felt so fortunate to have landed a job at Caldwell Elementary as a third-grade teacher right out of university. She had thoroughly enjoyed working with the children. It was the thing she had wanted to do since she was just a kid. She used to make Austin pretend to be her student. The memory made her smile.

A few years after landing her dream job, she'd met Pete. He had just started running his father's development company. Mr. Harris, Anthony, had built a great company, but Pete was taking it to the next level. He'd been so excited. Life had been really good for them.

After only six months together, they had decided to take the next step. There had been much talk about the wedding and the honeymoon, but she and Pete had decided to keep it simple. They'd had a lovely ceremony at the county park and rented a remote cottage on the water only a few miles away. They would have their few days of solitude and then get back to the business of their busy lives. They had the rest of their lives for traveling the world.

Except they didn't.

The first night at the cottage, two intruders broke in and woke them from deep sleep. It was late, and she and Pete had been drinking champagne—it was their wedding night, after all. The intruders had immediately drugged them. Rory closed her eyes against the memory of the things the intruders had done. Horrible…terrible things. And when they left, Pete was dead.

They had taken both their cell phones and the keys to Pete's SUV, so she'd had no way to call for help or to drive into town. In a near comatose state, she had held Pete for hours, just rocking his body as if by sheer power of will she could bring him back. She had no idea how much time passed. She hoped the drug meant that Pete hadn't felt the horrors done to him.

Eventually, she had recognized that it was necessary to leave him. First she had run from house to house on the short waterfront street. There were only a few, and all had been dark. No cars. No one answered the doors. So she had done the only thing left to do. She walked toward town in the hope that a car would come along. She'd been half naked, the nightgown she'd bought for her wedding night ripped. But the worst was the blood. She'd held Pete for all those hours. Blood had soaked into her gown…her skin.

Sometime in the wee hours of that morning, a car had driven past her stumbling journey along the road. The driver had stopped and called 9-1-1. She had been so grateful when the police arrived. Finally, someone to help.

But it was too late, of course. Pete was dead. The scene in the cottage had been like the big black moment in a horror movie.

At first everyone had been so kind to her…so helpful. Lulu and Austin had stayed at her side. Even Pete's parents had stood vigil with them as Rory healed and the investigation got underway.

But then, a mere two weeks later, all that changed because the police found nothing—not one single shred of evidence to back up Rory's story. There were no other prints in the cottage except hers and Pete's. The place had just been painted and thoroughly cleaned when they rented it. The only prints on the big kitchen knife used on Pete were hers. There were no close neighbors near the property. No one to hear them screaming. There were no tracks to show another vehicle had come into the parking area other than the one they drove. There simply was nothing to prove the story she conveyed.

The way folks looked at her then was something she recalled vividly from her childhood. She'd been called a witch, a demon child…all sorts of ugly names. Mostly because of the way she looked. Her hair was so dark and her eyes so light, not to mention her skin was so, so pale. Lulu's hippie vibe that had quickly rubbed off on Rory had added fuel to the fire. Kids at school had picked on her to no end.

She had thought all of that was behind her…until Pete's murder.

At trial, no one—not the jury or those watching from the gallery—saw anything beyond the dozens of her handprints in his blood. Everything else had faded into the background.

How in the world would the Colby Agency find the truth two years later when no one had found a single shred the day after? How could she prove that she had not killed the man she loved…that she was not the monster the media had dubbed her?

The *Murder Bride*.

Chapter Two

Kindred Residence
Tupelo Pike
Scottsboro, 5:30 p.m.

Rory had spent an hour walking around the backyard. The yard wasn't that large, but she'd spent a good deal of that time weeding flower beds and just admiring the many things her aunt had planted over the years. She had owned this place since she was about Rory's age. There was a lifetime of Lulu here.

For Rory it felt good to be outside and to breathe the warm air without fear of who might come after her or that her time outside her cold, austere cell was almost up. Freedom smelled and tasted better than almost anything.

As good as this felt, she reminded herself this freedom was only temporary. There were already hearings happening to determine if she was a flight risk. Her attorney, Gerald Patterson, had insisted in his last phone call to her that she needn't worry.

But she did and would.

You didn't lose everything when you had done nothing wrong and learn to trust again easily. She wasn't sure she would ever trust anyone other than Austin again. She had trusted Lulu, of course, but Lulu was gone.

The sound of a car turning into the driveway had her hurrying back into the house. It was about time for the Colby Agency investigator to arrive, but she wanted to be sure before going around front. Again, it was the trust thing. In the living room, a quick peek out the window confirmed she had made the right decision.

A convertible sports car had parked in her driveway. Two men hopped out and headed for her door.

Rory drew back from the window. Her gaze flew to the new dead bolt. It was locked, as was the other lock. Should she call the police?

She rolled her eyes. Like they would come. And even if they did, somehow it would be turned around and made to appear her fault.

A bang on the door made her jump.

"We know you're in there," a deep male voice warned. "You don't have to open the door or come out. We just want to give you a message."

A sudden blast of fury obliterating her fear, she unlocked the door and yanked it open, then she pushed open the screen door, forcing the two to step back. She looked from one to the other. Cade Coleman and Ronnie Smith. Both lifelong friends of Pete's.

"I'm listening." She looked from Cade to Ronnie.

Both men stared at her as if they'd lost their collective nerve, or maybe they were just so startled that she would risk opening the door they couldn't remember what they'd come to say.

"You're not going to get away with what you did," Ronnie warned. "One way or the other, we'll see that you don't."

Rory stepped past the screen door, let it slam behind her. "What will you do, Ronnie? Kill me? Is that what you believe Pete would want you to do?"

"Don't even say his name," Cade growled. "You lost that right when you murdered him."

Rory flinched. "Well, we agree on one thing." She stared the former high school football star in the eyes. "He was murdered all right, but it was a couple of guys—like the two of you—who did it." She looked from one to the other. "Maybe even friends of his."

Fury whipped across Cade's face. "You better watch your mouth—that kind of thing can get you dead."

Her heart pounded so hard she could barely breathe… but that beating in her chest was the only thing that told her she was alive anymore. Otherwise, she had died two years, one month and four days ago…the same night as her husband. The husband she did not…would not…could not have hurt, much less murdered.

"Don't waste your time," she said, the bravado draining away, defeat taking its place. "I'm already dead."

She turned her back on the two and went inside. She didn't even lock the door. What was the point? If those two wanted to storm her house, she couldn't stop them. Maybe she wouldn't even try.

Raised voices drew her back to the window. A Jackson County police cruiser had pulled into her driveway next to the convertible. The deputy was yelling at the two men. Rory couldn't determine who he was since his back was turned to her. But she hadn't called the police.

She shook her head. Ronnie and Cade would assume she had. Great. Now the two would be even angrier.

Cade spun out of her driveway, spraying gravel. What a fool. The one thing Rory knew with complete certainty was that Pete would be ashamed of his friends. Angry too. He would never have allowed anyone to talk to her that way.

But Pete was gone.

A knock on her door had her jumping again.

She pressed a hand to her chest and went to the window. The deputy—surprise flared inside her as she recognized him as Shane Carter, Pete's cousin—was standing at her door.

Fingers fumbling, she quickly unlocked and opened it. For a moment, she stared at the man through the screen door.

Then he drew it open. "Hey, Rory."

"Shane." She wanted to be glad to see him, but she wasn't sure why he was here or where he stood about what happened. He was part of Pete's family, and they blamed Rory. Hated Rory. Had done all in their power to put her away for good. One had even pushed for the death penalty.

"I told Cade and Ronnie I'd better not catch them here harassing you again."

As much as she appreciated what he'd done, she was confused. "Did someone call you?" She had no close neighbors, but she supposed someone driving by could have noticed the drama.

"No." He shook his head, stared at the floor a moment. "I heard you were coming home today, and I figured it would be best if I drove by occasionally while I'm on duty. You're right inside the city limits, out of my jurisdiction, but I figured just seeing an official vehicle would help ward off troublemakers."

She nodded slowly. "Thank you." She shrugged then. "I don't mean to sound ungrateful, but I guess I'm trying to figure out why you would care."

He met her gaze then. "I've done a lot of thinking over the past two years, and I think what happened to you is wrong. Plain wrong. Back then…" He looked away a moment. "It was all too fresh. Everyone was too hurt… too angry to think straight. And I was still in training. But two-plus years is long enough to realize that maybe things weren't the way they seemed. And I've had some experience on the job." He shrugged. "I see things a little different now."

Hope swelled in her chest. "Does anyone else in the family feel the way you do?"

He exhaled a big breath. "Not that I know of. Sorry. They still see things the way they did back then. Around town the talk is mixed. Some folks believe what the jury decided was right. Others think you were telling the truth. But those folks don't speak up to just anyone. You know how it is. The Harris family owns everything around here. If you take a side that's not theirs, then you could lose a job or have a loan recalled."

Which basically meant nothing had changed in this town. No surprise there. It was a small town, and when one family owned or had a big stake in the places that provided jobs or loaned money, it was difficult to speak your mind.

"Well, I guess they'll get another chance to make me look like the monster they believe I am." What could she do? Nothing except fight through the legal system that had failed her from the beginning. She had no other options.

Shane reached out and gave her arm a squeeze. "You're no monster. Anyone who knows you is aware of that."

She almost snorted out loud. Where were all those people when she needed them? No need to go there. She knew how things worked around here. Honestly, if she'd had any other option when she was released, she would have gone as far away from here as possible.

But she had nothing. No home if not for her aunt's generosity. No money in the bank except for the same. No job or possibilities of one. Nothing. Not to mention she had to be on hand for the new investigation.

The radio attached to Shane's shoulder sounded off. He responded, then flashed her a smile. "I gotta go." He reached into his shirt pocket and pulled out a folded piece of paper. He offered it to her. "This is my cell number. Call me if you need me." He shrugged again. "If there's any trouble, I'll come as fast as I can."

She accepted the paper. "Thank you, Shane."

"Good to see you," he said before taking off.

Rory watched him drive away. She wanted to feel like this was a good sign. Maybe an indication that at least some attitudes toward her had changed. But that required trust, and she just couldn't go there yet.

A black sedan slowed and made the turn into her driveway. The car parked, and the driver's side door opened.

This was most likely Chance Rader, the Colby Agency investigator. She sure hoped so. She was ready to get the initial meeting over and move forward with whatever plan he had developed.

When the man emerged from the driver's door, she recognized him. Tall, broad-shouldered, dark hair with a classically handsome face. None of which mattered as far as his credentials were concerned. But she had eyes, and his description was his description. She waved, pushed a smile into place.

He waved back. "I finally made it," he called to her. "Traffic was backed up on 565. Slowed me down."

"That's Huntsville. Always a traffic jam somewhere."

She hugged her arms around herself. Though Austin had brought her jeans and a nice pullover for changing into when they left the prison, she still felt the smell and the aura of the place clinging to her skin. Maybe she should have gotten in the shower as soon as she arrived home, but she hadn't wanted to have Austin waiting around with her shut up in the bathroom, and then being outside had been too tempting.

Chance Rader grabbed a bag, like a canvas-style briefcase, from the front passenger seat, then started in her direction. He didn't speak again until he had climbed the steps up to the porch. He thrust out his free hand. "It's nice to finally meet you in person."

Rory shook his hand, managed another smile. "Nice to meet you."

His palm was rougher than she'd expected. A little callused. As if he worked with wood or spent a lot of time in a garden. Not the smooth palm of someone who spent all his time in an office shuffling paper and absorbed in conference calls.

"Come in." She turned back to the door and walked into her house. Sounded strange to call it *her* house. Really, it would always be Lulu's home. He paused just inside the door, glanced around. "Would you like something to drink?" she asked. "Water? A soft drink?"

"I'm good. Thanks." He closed the door.

"You want to sit in here," she gestured to the sofa and chair that stood in the center of the small living room, "or at the kitchen table?"

He held up his briefcase. "The table would work better, I think."

"Sure."

Rory led the way to the kitchen. Like the rest of the

house, it was really small, with a table and four chairs in the center. She pulled out a chair and sat. Chance did the same on the other side of the table. No matter that she was well aware of all the steps the agency intended to take, and she was prepared to work with this investigator. Her nerves were jangling. *Deep breath. Stay calm and focus.*

He slid open the zipper on his soft-sided briefcase. "I realize this is all happening fast." He removed a file folder and placed it on the table, then tucked his briefcase into an empty chair. "You just got home, and I'm sure your head is spinning. But it's important we move quickly. We want to stay ahead in this investigation."

"I understand." She clasped her hands in her lap. At least this go-around she wasn't alone. Wait, that wasn't fair. Last time Austin and Lulu had been firmly on her side. The two had been with her every step of the way. No question. But this time she had real experts on her side. It would, she hoped, make all the difference.

Part of her resisted holding out any sort of hope. She waffled between believing the effort was pointless and futile and daring to hope exposing the truth was possible. She wanted that truth found. She really did. More for Pete than for herself. Certainly for Austin. If she was finally free again, that was just the icing on the cake.

Chance opened the file folder and showed her the top page. It was a bullet list. She scanned the words there.

"This," he explained, "is a list of what I hope to accomplish with you. It's not written in stone and is absolutely open to any change you feel needs to be made. But it's a basic map of what we need to do."

Rory scanned the list, her gaze stopping on one point in particular. Her stomach knotted along with her fingers.

She moistened her lips. "I'll be honest, I'm not thrilled about going back to the scene."

"I understand." His eyes told her he meant the words. "But it's important that we make sure nothing was missed."

"But it's been over two years." What he was suggesting seemed a total waste of time.

"It has been a long while, but that doesn't mean we might not find something the others missed. It happens years after in some cases. Evidence that was missed has been found twenty years after an event. In some cases, even longer, I'm sure. We don't want to overlook any possibility. Plus, there is always the possibility that a new memory will be prompted."

She nodded. "Okay." Rory's dread wasn't going to be the reason this effort failed. However difficult it was, she would do whatever necessary.

"You and I will go over everything you recall from the days and weeks prior to what happened. We'll talk to people—or try to."

"I won't hold my breath on getting anywhere with anyone who might have information about that night. But we can try." She thought of Shane and what he'd said. "Just before you arrived, Shane Carter, Pete's cousin, stopped by. He's a county deputy now. He told me some folks might be more open to my side of the story. But we'll see."

"You have his number?"

She nodded. "He said I could call anytime."

"Do you trust him?"

There was the real question. She might as well get this part over with. She unknotted her hands and forced her body to relax. She looked directly at the man who had been sent to help her. He seemed like a very nice man. Brown hair, neatly trimmed. Thick and full. Deeper brown eyes. Kind eyes. Handsome for sure—as she had noticed before. He was exactly what her mind might conjure when she thought about young private investigators and detectives in the movies or in books. And based on his agency's reputation, there was every reason to believe in his work and to trust him. Except…she couldn't.

"I have a problem with trust." She looked away a moment. "Since that night and then the trial, I was so let down. So disappointed. I feel like I can't trust anyone." She met his gaze once more. "I recognize your agency's reputation, and by extension, yours is reliable— outstanding to say the least. Because of that, I will cooperate fully with you. I will do all possible to try and prove I'm telling the truth. I'll defer to your lead as we go. But right now, I just can't trust anyone." She searched his eyes for understanding. "Not even you."

He smiled—which surprised her. Crossed his arms and braced them on the table. "Rory, after what you've been through, I would be stunned if you trusted me. We will work together to get the job done—just as you said. But I don't expect anything more. At any time if you feel overwhelmed or worried, maybe scared, all you have to do is say so. I'll stop whatever I'm doing, and we'll work it out. You have my word."

Air filled her lungs, and she realized she had been holding her breath. "That works."

"Good. Remember, this is not only about you, but also *for* you. I'm just the guy doing the legwork. Now, I'm leaving all this with you." He pushed the folder toward her. "You'll see the ways we want you to look back on what happened. You'll be surprised how many more details come to you if you look back from a different perspective. Even when it feels futile, it's important that you try. We understand how difficult it is, but it's crucial that you give it your best shot."

She glanced at the manila folder. "All right."

"I've booked a room at the motel just down the road where Tupelo Pike intersects with Willow Street."

Rory knew the one. A little low-rent, but it was the closest to her. She supposed that was his reasoning for the choice. "I know the place."

"Don't hesitate to call if you need anything at all. If there's trouble, you call me first, then 9-1-1."

For the past couple of days, she wasn't sure what she had expected. But this worked surprisingly fine. Felt far more relaxed than she had expected.

"I can stay and walk you through what you'll find in the folder," he offered, "but what I really want is for you to read everything over and see what comes to mind without any outside expectations or suggestions."

"I understand."

He stood. "All right then." He grabbed his briefcase. "I'll get out of your hair, and I'll pick you up for breakfast in the morning. Seven thirty sound okay to you?"

"Sure." A new kind of anticipation lit inside her. This was really happening.

At the front door, he paused. "We'll get this done, Rory. You'll see." He smiled, and then he was gone.

Rory closed and locked the door. She watched through the window as he drove away. She turned and leaned against the door. For a long while, she just stood there and thought about the fact that this would be her first night in a real bed—her bed in more than two years.

Her composure started to crumble. The tears spilled

over first. She struggled to steel herself so that she could hold them back, but that wasn't happening.

She cried. Her body shuddered so hard she put her arms around herself and held tightly. She felt so alone.

At first—after what happened—she had been in shock. Wounded and needing to heal, physically and emotionally. Then the new nightmare began—the investigation turned toward her as the murderer of her own husband. She had never been allowed to grieve Pete, not properly. She'd been in a fight for her life from her injuries and then from the investigation. Once she was in prison, she had lapsed into a flood of grief so overwhelming she still didn't know how she had survived it. Finally, she had reached that hollow place. The place where there were no more feelings, no more anything. There was only existing.

Now all those numbed feelings suddenly came rushing back. Loneliness. Fear. Uncertainty. Hope. Dear God, how long had it been since she dared to hope?

The Colby Agency was her only hope.

Chapter Three

Kindred Residence
Tupelo Pike
Scottsboro, 11:30 p.m.

Rory told herself she should be in bed by now, but there was something about being able to stay up as long as she liked—with the lights on. No one could tell her when the lights were to go off. No one could tell her when she could eat and when she couldn't. To that end, she had a snack cake, a soft drink and a bowl of popcorn on the coffee table in front of her. Also, scattered across the battered wood top was an empty snack cake wrapper as well as one that had held cheesy crackers. And the bowl of popcorn was half empty. To her credit, she also had a bottle of water.

She leaned back and groaned. She was stuffed. Couldn't eat another bite if her life depended on it. A smile spread across her lips. It was awesome. She patted her belly and reminded herself that she couldn't keep doing this for long. But tonight, if she were a drinker or a smoker, she would overindulge in those wicked activities as well. But she'd never been a smoker and not much of a drinker. Wine occasionally and the champagne on her wedding day.

Her smile wilted. Images from that day flashed rapid-fire through her mind like a good movie that suddenly turned bad on fast-forward. She pushed the painful images away, didn't want to look just now.

Pushing to her feet, she grabbed her cell phone and headed to the kitchen. She needed some air. She tucked her new cell phone into the pocket of the nightgown she'd dug out of one of Lulu's drawers. None of the clothes that Austin had brought had included sleepwear. Mr. and Mrs. Harris had probably burned everything else. Not that she would have wanted to sleep in anything she'd worn before…when Pete had slept beside her.

She shook off the thoughts. Didn't matter. She had worked really hard not to hold his parents' beliefs about her against them. Their son had been murdered, and the only evidence of who killed him pointed to Rory. Of course they hated her.

"Looking forward," she murmured, "not backward." At least for tonight. Dissecting every moment of that terrible time was necessary, but she didn't have to start tonight.

She slipped out the back door and sat down on the porch step. The air was cooler now that it was well after dark. She stared up at the moon and stars. The sight brought back her smile. She hadn't seen those in a long time. There had been no window in her cell. What little time she had been allowed outside was during the daylight hours. Funny how you didn't realize how much you would miss something until it was gone with no possibility of ever being available to you again. As if Nature had decided she needed the break, a shooting star flashed across the sky.

Rory smiled. Maybe this was a sign that everything really was going to be all right.

Glass shattered.

Rory shot to her feet and hurried to the back door. Listening for trouble, she slipped through the house, stalled at the front window. A white four-door pickup truck roared away, the sound fading in the night as it disappeared.

She froze, the remembered sound of shattering glass echoing in her mind.

The windows in the living room were all intact as far as she could see. She headed for the hall. The first room on the right was the one Austin had made into an office. She flipped the switch for the overhead light.

Broken glass glinted on the old hardwood floor. A big rock lay in the middle of it.

The window wasn't that large, but it was big enough to have made a mess.

"Damn it."

She retraced her steps to the kitchen. The broom hung on a nail by the back door as it always had. Dustpan sat on the floor, propped against the wall behind it. She grabbed both and headed back to the home office. The windows were old, so the glass had shattered in dozens of pieces big and small. Some shards remained in the sash like broken teeth.

"That's what happens when you let your guard down, Rory." Just when she'd started to relax, there was a reminder that she had no right to do so. She was the *Murder Bride*, and no one believed her story.

Time was required, but she finally swept all the shards into the dustpan without cutting herself. She shoved the rock into a corner with the broom, then emptied the glass into the kitchen garbage can, walked back to her new office and swept the room all over again. In her experience, you never got up all the broken glass the first time. Inevitably a piece would wind up in your foot. A round with the vacuum cleaner was next. It was old, and she wasn't sure how well it worked, but she gave it a try nonetheless.

When she was satisfied that she'd done all she could to clean up any remaining fragments, she grabbed her phone and the flashlight that stood on the counter next to the back door. Lulu had kept one there for as long as Rory could remember. Way before flashlight apps had been invented for cell phones.

She let herself out the back door and headed for the shed. Surely there was something out there she could use to secure the broken window. Lulu hadn't been one to let any sort of resource go to waste. She insisted that you never knew when you might need a piece of wood or odd screw or nail or whatever was left over from a project. Better to have it than not.

The shed was actually a good-sized garage, but there was no overhead door. The old-fashioned carriage-style doors no longer hung straight, but they did the job of protecting the interior well enough. Rory lifted the cross board that held them closed, and the doors swung open. She roved the beam of the flashlight over the interior. Lulu's ancient Volkswagen Beetle stood in the middle. Her aunt had hand-painted colorful flowers on the doors of the little sunny yellow car. She'd loved it as if it were her child. Rory would bet money that the bead necklaces still hung from the rearview mirror and fake flowers remained perched in the little dash vase.

She smiled as she thought of all the times she had been dropped off at school in that flashy bug. The other girls had been so envious of the car. Rory's wardrobe had been a different story. Church rummage sales and consignment shops had been the places Lulu shopped. Wearing second- or thirdhand clothes never bothered Rory. Well, maybe that once when the snobbiest girl in her class had recognized a dress as one she had cast off. Lulu had reminded Rory that the dress had been far too nice for such a mean girl and that she had looked far prettier in it anyway.

After some digging, Rory found a piece of plywood that looked to be about the right size. Lulu had no fancy battery-operated tools, but she did have an old circular saw and a drill, both of which plugged into an electric outlet.

"Better than trying to attach it by hand."

Rory found the right tip for the screwheads, then gathered the drill and the plywood and headed back to the house. She would have to come back out and close up the shed when she finished.

A loud engine roared in the distance. Rory stiffened, listened harder. Was it the same one? The white pickup whose occupant had thrown the rock? Surely they wouldn't come back.

Rather than risk being caught outside if the person or persons did return, she hurried into the house and locked the door. She made it into the home office and turned off the light in the room, then waited. Sound carried in the darkness. The truck could have been a mile or so away. No sooner than the thought occurred, headlights bobbed in the darkness.

The truck braked to a stop in her driveway. The distinct crunch of gravel pierced the air. Her heart thundered even harder. Voices echoed. At least two distinct voices were clear. Both male. The men apparently didn't care if they woke her.

A deep thud. She jumped. Something had hit the front of the house. Another thud…this time louder. She dared to ease closer to the window. It was too dark to tell for sure, but the two were holding something like…*guns.*

Fear spiraled through her body.

One jogged back to the truck and opened the passenger-side door. She held her breath. The interior light from the cab gave her a glimpse of what he carried.

Paintball gun?

He closed the truck door and returned to his friend. The thudding started again.

"You hiding in there?" one shouted.

Rory drew back from the window…baffled as to what to do. She didn't have a weapon. She didn't dare engage them. Maybe it was better to pretend she wasn't home or that she was asleep. But who could sleep through the bangs and thuds coming one after the other?

Not to mention the shouting and laughter.

She couldn't just stand here in the dark. She had to call someone. It was either the police or Chance Rader. She decided on Chance. She eased into the hall, crouched down and tapped his name in her contact list. She'd added his number to her phone even before he arrived at her house.

He answered on the first ring.

"I'm sorry to bother you," she whispered. "There are two men outside, and they're shooting at my house with what looks like paintball guns."

"I'll be right there."

"You better come out or we're coming in!" one of the men called.

The shouted words had her pulse racing.

"What was that?" Chance asked.

The sound of his vehicle starting in the background

of the call gave Rory some fraction of relief. It wouldn't take him long to get here. "They said if I don't come out, they're coming in."

"Call 9-1-1. I'm on the way."

Rory ended the call and did as he instructed. She provided her name and address and answered the necessary questions. Almost immediately she was told officers were en route. The dispatcher asked that she remain on the line until the officers arrived.

Rory squeezed her eyes shut and tried to block out the shouting and banging now happening at her front door. They had apparently run out of ammo for their paint guns.

"Come on out, bitch!" one of them shouted.

"Here comes the bride," the other singsonged, "all covered in blood!"

"How did it feel?" the first demanded.

More banging on the door had her certain it would fly open at any second.

"How did it feel," he repeated, "to kill your own husband…to have his blood all over you?"

The dispatcher was talking again, but Rory couldn't listen. The blood roaring in her ears and the sounds outside blocked out everything else. Were those men the same ones who had come by before? Cade and Ronnie? The ones who had thrown the rock?

They had to be drunk or high. Surely they didn't expect to get away with what they were doing.

Of course they believed they would get away with harassing her. She was the *Murder Bride*. She should still be in prison. The police would hate her even more for making them look bad.

A different kind of thud echoed next.

"What the hell?" a voice—one of the two paintball gun guys—demanded.

More sounds she couldn't quite distinguish…hollow and quieter but still thud-like noises.

She didn't dare move. Didn't dare say a word. The voice on the phone was asking her if she was all right, but she couldn't answer.

A knock on her door followed by, "Rory, it's Chance. You okay in there?"

She scrambled into a standing position, her legs nearly asleep from squatting so long. "I'm okay."

Evidently the dispatcher thought Rory was talking to her. She said, "The police should be arriving now."

"My friend is here now too," Rory said. "He's on the porch. I'm opening the door."

The dispatcher was telling Rory not to open the door just yet, but it was too late, she already had. Chance was there. On the porch, lying motionless, were the two men. Blue lights flashed on the street. A patrol car roared up behind Chance's car. Rory's knees went weak. She leaned against the nearest wall.

"They're here," she said to the dispatcher. "I'm on the front porch with my friend. The two men who were harassing me are down."

Rory didn't wait for her response. She ended the call.

"Put your hands up where they can see them," Chance said to her, his voice quiet.

Almost immediately one of the officers shouted those same instructions as he approached, weapon drawn.

She and Chance waited, hands up, until the two uniformed officers climbed the steps and visually assessed the situation.

"Ms. Harris?" The one who had shouted the order looked her up and down once more.

"Yes. I'm the one who called." She gestured to the guys face down on the porch. "Those are the men who were shooting paintballs at my house and shouting for me to come out."

The second officer had walked around the end of the house.

The one on the porch steps motioned to Chance with his flashlight. "Who's this?"

"Chance Rader," he said. "I'm a private investigator working for Ms. Harris. I'm staying at the motel down the street. She called and told me what was happening. I told her I was coming right over, but I suggested that she call you as well. When I arrived, the men were beating on the door and shouting profanities. I disabled them, and then we waited for you to arrive."

"Are you armed, Mr. Rader?" the officer asked.

"I am not."

The officer shifted his attention to Rory. "Are you armed, ma'am?"

"No, and there are no weapons in my house."

Discounting the kitchen knives that had belonged to her aunt. Rory felt sick at the idea that the police would likely use that against her somehow if they searched the house.

The officer handed something to Chance. "Make yourself useful, Mr. Rader, and secure those two."

"My pleasure."

"Ma'am, why don't you turn on some lights?"

Rory nodded and reached inside to flip the switch. Chance was crouched next to the first of the two men. He secured his hands behind his back. The second man started to rouse. He kicked at Chance.

The officer crouched down at his head. "Well, well, if it's not Riley O'Brien. Looks like you got yourself into a little trouble tonight."

O'Brien shouted obscenities at the officer.

Chance stepped back from the other man he had secured. That one too had roused and was attempting to get onto his knees.

The officer instructed him to stay down, and the man started shouting that he hadn't done anything. The second officer reappeared.

"Let's load 'em up," the officer who sounded in charge said. Rory and Chance waited on the porch while the two men who had caused the disturbance were loaded into the back seat of the cruiser. One officer stayed in the patrol car while the other, the one who'd done all the talking, returned to the porch. As he approached, he scanned his flashlight over her house. Varying sizes of red splats dotted the faded and chipped white paint.

"Looks like you've got yourself a new design theme."

Rory felt sick. "A broken window too."

"Let's go inside," the office suggested, "and I'll take your statement. Then I'll get these two back to the station and processed."

Rory went inside first, then Chance. They settled on the sofa, and the officer took the chair. As Rory recounted the details of what happened starting with her broken window, she noticed that his name was Proctor. She'd gone to middle school with a boy with the last name Proctor. The officer actually looked a bit like that kid. She wondered if it was the same guy. He'd moved to a different town before high school. If it was him, he was likely wondering how one of his former classmates had become a convicted murderer.

When the interview was finished, Officer Proctor stood. "We'll have a tow truck come for the vehicle." He tucked his pen into his pocket and did the same with his notepad. "O'Brien still lives with his parents. I'm sure they'll see to it that the damages are taken care of to prevent any criminal charges."

And that was the way of it in small towns. Guys like the two who had vandalized her home and terrorized her somehow never faced the consequences of their actions. But to argue the idea would be pointless. She had enough trouble as it was.

"Thank you." She rose to her feet. "I appreciate you coming out."

He gave her a nod and headed for the door. She followed. He paused before going out and looked back at her. "You don't remember me, do you?"

She mustered up her best effort at a smile. "You remind me of someone I went to school with. Seventh grade, I think."

"That's me." He glanced at Chance, then set his attention on her once more. "I just moved back last year. Sorry to hear about your trouble. But just so you know, there are a lot of folks in this town who believe you don't deserve to be out of prison. Watch your back." Again he hesitated. "But that doesn't mean everyone feels that way."

He left. Rory watched from the door as the patrol car drove away. She wanted to feel marginally better in light of his comment, but as sure as she did, something else would happen. Instead, she let it go and locked the door.

"This has been a tough day," Chance said, reading her mind.

She nodded, tears burning her eyes. She refused to cry. Damn it. But now that the disturbance was over, at least this time, she felt weak with the weight of the coming retrial. Devastated at the inevitability of how this was obviously going to continue. How had she ever believed for a second that she could come back here and prove her innocence, much less have a life?

"There are people who will initially try to make you regret standing up for yourself," the man watching her so closely said gently. "In any case like this, it's always the same. People do stupid things. Sometimes because they firmly believe they're right, other times just to be a part of something. But in my experience, as the details start to emerge, these things generally come to a quick end." He shrugged, offered her a smile. "It's a small town. You're the latest big news. Give it time to settle."

She drew in a big breath. "I wish I wasn't…news, I mean."

"I wish you weren't either." He hitched his head toward the hall. "How about we get that window situation taken care of and call it a night. I'd prefer to stay on your sofa, just in case, if that's okay with you."

His suggestion had relief washing over her. "That is very okay with me."

She hadn't expected to be afraid…to need someone to babysit her. But maybe she had been a fool to believe she could be here—in this town where it all happened—and no one would make a big deal out of her challenge to the court's past decision. Unquestionably she had expected the Harris family to snub her. To talk about her when interviewed by the media, on social media and in plain old local gossip. To try and make her look even worse. But she really hadn't expected this sort of behavior out of people not related to her dead husband. Pete would never have wanted his friends to do these things.

She kept telling herself this, but Pete wasn't here. Someone had murdered him, and for all she knew, it could have been friends of his. Someone jealous of who he was and what he had accomplished—of his family's money. Her attorney had brought up the idea to her during the trial. At the time she had been so devastated she really hadn't been able to think straight, much less form a coherent scenario about murder.

But she'd had plenty of time to think in prison. She'd also seen and heard enough horror to understand that people—most people—were capable of very bad things when pushed into a corner or prompted in just the right way.

Together she and Chance boarded up the broken window. She would get it repaired eventually. Right now, she had far more pressing issues. He took the tools back to the shed and secured the doors while she rounded up a quilt and pillow for him.

When he returned to the house, she noticed for the first time that he only wore a tee and jeans. He'd hurried to come to her rescue. She was grateful.

"Thank you. For whatever you did out there." She laughed, the sound bubbling up from her throat unexpectedly. "You were like some sort of ninja. Those guys didn't stand a chance."

He chuckled. "Nothing new or original—certainly nothing ninja-like. The two were making so much noise I had the element of surprise." A shrug lifted his broad shoulders. "The fact that they were both inebriated made it considerably easier."

She passed him the pillow and quilt. It wasn't until her arms were empty that she realized she had gone through this whole ordeal in her aunt's vintage nightgown that sported a Smoke More Weed logo.

Rory crossed her arms over her chest and the faded letters. "Well, thank you again. I really appreciate…" How did she even describe this?

"You don't need to thank me, Rory. I'm here to help."

She nodded, felt that choking sensation again. She was so tired of the emotions and the urge to cry. "Good night then."

"Good night."

Rory headed to her room. She couldn't wait to climb into bed and turn off her brain.

If only the dreams didn't come.

But they would. They always did.

Chapter Four

Tuesday, June 16

Kindred Residence
Tupelo Pike
Scottsboro, 7:00 a.m.

The coffee had brewed, the rich scent filling the small kitchen.

Chance had been up since before six. He had walked around the property. Checked the tree line. The area was well wooded to be so close to town. Only a few miles up the road was the intersection where his motel was, and near that area, things were far more densely populated with businesses.

He'd found no issues outside. No indication of new trouble. Nothing except the splats of red that dotted the front of the small house Rory called home. A good pressure washing would likely take care of that problem. If he'd been able to locate a water hose, he would have taken care of the mess as soon as he got up. But there was no water hose or scrub brush or anything else that would help with the task. They could pick something up when they went out today. Leaving Rory at home alone was ob viously not doable under the circumstances. They would need to discuss the issue at some point today. Staying at his motel, even as close as it was, might not be the best option for her safety given the level of animosity directed at her in the space of only a few hours.

He poured a cup of coffee and leaned against the counter. If she was willing and emotionally up to the challenge, he wanted to visit the crime scene today. The sooner they got that difficult task behind them, the better. The agency had rented the cottage where the nightmare took place for the week, so there was plenty of time if today wasn't good for Rory. His concern was that the police would suddenly decide to take possession of the property for their own purposes.

With a long draw of his coffee, he considered what others saw when they looked at Rory. He'd read all the statements and interviews associated with her case. Some—clearly not friends—had mentioned Rory being called a witch back in school. Her really dark black hair and incredibly light blue eyes were unusual for sure. Her skin was inordinately pale, and her build was slight. Yet her voice was strong. Her determination remarkable. All those contrasts made for a rare combination. Add to the mix her bohemian aunt, and Rory had been called many things in her young life—witch was likely the nicest of all those unkind terms.

But as an adult, she'd proven herself by landing a teaching position at a local elementary school and being honored as teacher of the year her second term. Her involvement with the son of one of the town's wealthiest and most prominent families had set her life on a different path. She'd become a respected member of Scottsboro society.

Until the wedding.

Everyone around her—except her brother and aunt—had turned on her. She'd been fired from her job. Found guilty of murdering her husband and called the most vile name—the *Murder Bride*. Some, in their statements, had gone so far as to suggest they had always thought that perhaps she'd set the fire that killed her parents.

Chance had dug up the file on that long-ago house fire. Arson had never been suspected. The house was an older one with two fireplaces. One cold spring night, the fire the father had started hadn't completely died down before they went to bed. Rory's parents had awakened to the house in flames. The smoke and confusion had them searching desperately for their children when they were exactly where they were supposed to be—in their beds. The father found Rory and carried her out, then went back in for Austin. When he emerged with the boy, he realized his wife hadn't come out. He went back in to find her, and the two never came out. An elderly neighbor had witnessed the frantic desperation. What happened had not been anyone's fault. A simple, deadly mistake.

"Good morning."

His attention shifted back to the here and now. Rory stood in the doorway. He smiled. "Good morning." He gestured to the counter. "Coffee's ready."

"Thank you." She walked in his direction. "I hope you slept okay on that lumpy sofa."

"I slept just fine. Thank you." The truth was he never slept well when on assignment. Knowing someone else's safety and future depended on him was always at the forefront of his thoughts, and sound sleep didn't work well with being on alert for the slightest shift in the environment.

As she poured her coffee, he couldn't help watching her delicate fingers work. She was like a fine porcelain doll. How had she ever survived prison for two minutes, much less nearly two years?

She settled at the small table in the center of the room. "How do we start?"

He joined her at the table, taking the chair opposite her. "There are certain aspects of the case that we should cover first. The detective reopening the investigation will be moving quickly—if he's any good at all. If we can prevent it, we don't need to let him get ahead of us."

"Makes sense." She sipped her coffee.

He sure hoped she would understand the necessity of what he was about to propose. "It's important that our first move is a visit to where the murder happened."

Her eyes widened with something like disbelief. "We have to do that now? Today?"

"It's imperative, yes," he confirmed. "I wouldn't ask otherwise. And although the agency has rented the cottage for the week, we can't be sure at what moment the police will step in and reseal it as a crime scene for the purposes of their investigation. If that happens, it will be difficult—maybe impossible—to get in."

A slow, vague nod, then, "Okay. If that's what it takes, then I can get through it."

There was that determination he'd noted in what he'd read about her background. "Good."

She studied him a moment, her face clouded with uncertainty as if trying to articulate what was on her mind. Finally, she said, "I don't want to sound as if I'm doubting your decisions about how to proceed, but it's been a little over two years. Really, what do you expect to find? If the police didn't find any evidence in the days immediately following what happened, how can you expect to at this point?"

He wasn't sure his explanation would set her any more at ease. "It's not as much about what we might find as far as physical evidence as it is about what you might remember by being in the place where it happened."

She drew back a little. "I told the police everything I remembered. The drug those…men used left me in sort of a brain fog. In and out of consciousness." She shook her head. "I can't imagine recalling anything new now."

The drug, Rohypnol, used the way it was—injected—could have killed them both. During trial, the prosecutor had gone so far as to suggest Rory had a drug problem and that maybe she had drugged her husband. It was possible, they had claimed, that it was the drugs that caused the night to turn violent. The scenario had been presented as if the husband had realized what his wife had done and grown upset, and she may have lashed out more violently than intended. Not impossible, Chance mused, but highly unlikely.

"But you might," he countered, shifting his thoughts back to the here and now. "All it takes is one little thing to turn the case around."

She closed her eyes, drew in a big breath, then let it out. "You—" she opened her eyes once more "—don't understand. I have dreamed about what happened nearly every night for the past two years. It is always the same…always exactly what I told the police back then."

"The mind has a way of protecting itself," he explained. "Sometimes there are things our brains hold back to prevent the pain we might not be able to tolerate. Other times, that hidden thing only needs a little prompt or a little time to push it out where we can see it. Going there, walking in the room…touching the things you touched that night might trigger a memory you buried so deep that it has never surfaced even in your dreams."

She held his gaze for a long moment, and he was startled all over again by the barely there shade of blue. "As much as I wish it didn't," she admitted, "what you say makes sense."

"We can grab breakfast en route," he offered, "if you're prepared to go now."

"Sure." She finished off her coffee and took the cup to the sink.

He checked the back door and secured the dead bolt, while she gathered her phone and went to the front door. He met her there, waited for her to go out first. Once they were down the porch steps, she surveyed the damage to the house.

She winced. "God, that's pretty awful."

"We can clean it up when we get back. We'll need to stop for a few things, but it shouldn't be that difficult." He turned his attention to the window. "The window will be a little more complicated. We'll have to find a shop that can cut the glass to the proper size. A little glazing putty, and that'll do it."

"Sounds like a good plan." She turned and headed for his car.

She wasn't convinced that any amount of work would *do it*, he suspected. Not when it came to her life. He got how she would feel that way. It was really hard to put your life back together when others kept knocking you down. She had been knocked down at every turn after her husband's murder.

Just maybe, he could change that. For today, he would

settle for a single glimmer of tangible hope she could grab on to.

In the end it would take more than hope to turn this situation around. Especially when logic dictated there was no doubt someone out there who didn't want the story to change.

Chapter Five

White Cottage
Scenic Drive
Hollywood, Alabama, 8:50 a.m.

Rory's skin felt as if ants were crawling all over her. She needed to move…to do something. But all she could do was stare through the windshield at the chalet-style cottage in front of her.

Chance had parked and shut off the engine, but he'd said nothing yet.

She understood. He wanted her to focus on her thoughts, not his voice or his questions. Her feelings and the sensations related to being back here for the first time since that night were what he wanted to hear about.

Her wedding night.

Rory shivered at the memory. This was something she hadn't believed she would ever need to do again. But, as he said, it was likely necessary. Could possibly even prove helpful. So she would endure the hurt and just do it.

On their wedding day, she and Pete had arrived in his SUV. He'd parked right where they were sitting now. Rory closed her eyes. Her brand-new husband had leaned across the console and pulled her into a deep kiss. And then another and another. He'd whispered between kisses, warning her of all the things he intended to do to her. She had giggled and whispered her own deepest desires and erotic intentions.

They'd climbed out of the SUV and rushed to the door of the charming cottage he'd chosen for their honeymoon. They were already tugging each other's clothes off before they'd so much as gotten through the door. The frantic, breathless sounds echoed through her mind as if she were back there…smelling his scent, tasting his lips and his skin.

Hours later they'd come back outside and grabbed their bags. The moon had been big and bright. The moment had felt magical. Nothing else mattered. The whole world had felt a million miles away. It was just the two of them.

Rory opened her eyes. "When we came back outside to get our bags," she said, turning to the man behind the steering wheel, "I don't think we locked the cottage door. I'm not even sure we locked it when we first arrived and went inside. Or the second time we went inside."

He acknowledged her words with a nod.

She reached for the car door and got out. Glimpses of that night—laughter, stolen kisses and touches—flickered one after the other through her head. They had meandered along the path to the door, which was actually the back door of the cottage. The front faced the lake. She paused at the door and studied it.

Chance lingered a few steps behind her.

Her fingers traced the brass welcome sign on the door. Giggles whispered in her head as she recalled Pete trying to open the door without taking his hands off her body. They had lived together for months already, and still they had been crazy for the taste and feel of each other.

Chance reached around her to enter the code for unlocking the door. She stared at him, her heart pounding, her throat too tight for speech. She felt too warm, and at the same time, ice crept a slow path through her veins. He pushed the door inward, and she walked inside. More of those whispers sifted through her, making the organ in her chest beat even faster.

The door closed behind her, and she jumped.

Rory turned to face the man who'd brought her here. "We didn't lock the door. I'm sure of it." She closed her eyes, forced those moments to replay in her head. Pete's arms had been around her. They had half walked, half stumbled to the bedroom, leaving their bags on the floor by the door.

"We had gone out to get our bags. It was late." She shook her head. "I don't remember what time."

"Did you come back to the door for your bags before the intruders showed up?"

Her forehead was lined with the effort of searching her brain. "Yes. We must have. Because I was wearing a nightgown when they…broke in."

"Let's walk to the bedroom you used," Chance suggested.

She met his gaze, held it for a time. As much as she wanted to argue with the suggestion, she turned and started forward. The door entered the cottage near the kitchen. The bedroom was just to the right…only a few steps. The bedroom, like the rest of the place, was white. The walls, the floors…everything was white with only a piece of furniture or decor that deviated from the pure white. Even the exterior was all white, thus the name White Cottage.

The bed wasn't large because the room wasn't. The

cottage was small. Built like a chalet with steep vaulted ceilings and enormous windows. It was beautiful, simple and utterly charming. When Pete saw how enamored she was with the place, he insisted he would build her a lake house just like this one.

"*Cottage*," she had argued. "*This is a cottage*."

He had laughed and conceded the point.

"This is where you were when the intruders arrived," Chance said.

She nodded. "We were asleep. We'd had a lot of champagne."

"Was the television turned on?"

A small television sat on the chest of drawers next to the French doors that led to the balcony. She shook her head. "No. No television."

"What about music?"

"We'd had music on earlier, but the battery on his cell phone had died, and we hadn't bothered to dig out the charger. So no music was playing when I woke up."

Rory walked to the French doors and stared out over the water below. It was so calm and peaceful. There were no houses on the other side of the lake. There were a few neighbors along this side, but most were rental properties, and none had been occupied that night.

She turned to Chance. "Is it strange that on a Friday night in May, there wasn't a single other rented property on this street?" Not once in two years had she considered the idea. But now, looking back, it seemed odd.

"Let's sit down and discuss what you remember about the other houses."

Rory led the way to the main living area. It too was small. Just a sofa, side tables and a dining table. The space was connected to the galley kitchen. Just a modest rectangle with those same cathedral ceilings. An iron spiral staircase at the other end led to a loft.

She sat down on the sofa while Chance pulled a chair from the table so he could sit facing her without, she assumed, crowding her too much.

"The wedding was at six on a Friday." She smiled, thinking back. "We were so busy. We'd considered waiting until later in the summer and taking a real honeymoon in the Bahamas or something like that, but we couldn't wait. In the end, we decided to keep it simple. There would be plenty of time for more lavish vacations."

Except there hadn't been time.

"So you arrived here about what time?"

No doubt he was aware of all these details from her statement in the case file, but she understood that he wanted her to revisit those details in hopes of sparking a new memory. Maybe he was on to something, because she had remembered not locking the door and the oddity of none of the other rentals in the little cove being occupied.

"Wait…" A frown tugged at her lips. "The detective— Fowler, Detective Raymond Fowler—said if there had been intruders, then surely there would have been evidence the door had been tampered with." Her gaze collided with Chance's. "But if we didn't lock the door, then that wouldn't be the case."

"Excellent point," he agreed. "Think about when you rushed out to find help. Do you recall if the door was damaged in some way? Did you have to stop and open it, or was it already open?"

Rory closed her eyes and summoned that painful memory. She had carefully lowered Pete to the floor. She'd been sitting on the floor holding him for a very long time. Hours surely. Just rocking back and forth with him leaned against her chest. She'd gotten up and walked to the door. She remembered looking back several times. Then she'd been outside.

"I think…" She replayed the memory again. "No." She shook her head. "I know I did not open the door when I left, so it had to be open already."

"You walked out into the darkness," he said, prompting her to go on.

"It was cool. The moon was big…like last night." She blinked, prodding her brain for more. "I remember wrapping my arms around myself…and the stones." Her toes curled in her shoes. "No, not stones, gravel. The gravel was jabbing at my feet because I hadn't put on my shoes."

By the time a driver had come along, her feet had been bruised, the flesh ruptured by the gravel and rocks and whatever else she had stepped on.

"I went to the left first. I rushed from house to house. There were no lights on anywhere. No cars…just Pete's SUV. I banged on all the doors, but no one answered. Later the detective said no one was home at any of the other rentals at the time." She settled her attention once more on the man watching her. "Then I ran for a while. To River Drive and… I just kept going until there were headlights."

"Before you left this street," he said, "did you hear anything? Sound carries at night. Maybe cars on a road farther away? Dogs? Anything at all?"

She struggled to find a snippet of memory that included some sort of sound. "No. I don't remember anything." She frowned. "There was this hollow sound in my head. The echo of my own breath…the pounding in my chest."

"What did you smell? Smoke? It was a cool night. Maybe from a chimney. Or the lingering odor of an outdoor firepit that had been used earlier in the night. Exhaust from a car."

"Just that earthy smell after rain." Her brow furrowed as she searched her memories. "It had rained, I guess. I remember my feet were damp."

"There was no mention of rain in the case file reports."

"Maybe it only rained a little, but it rained. I distinctly remember my feet were wet." She sat up straighter. "The detective insisted it hadn't rained, but I was certain it had."

"Easy enough to find out." He pulled out his cell phone and started a search.

The memory of rushing along the street scrolled through her mind. "There are bigger houses on River Drive. I remember seeing them in my peripheral vision, but I didn't stop. I guess because no one had been home at the ones here, I was sure no one would be at any of those either. They were all dark. But it was late. People were probably just in bed. All I could think about was running until I found my way back to town...to help."

She remembered the determination and desperation to find help...it eclipsed all other thought. Even rational thought.

"You're right." He looked up from his phone. "Hollywood got one tenth of an inch of rain that night. Not much but enough that if you went outside immediately after it stopped, the grass and pavement would have been wet."

That was at least two things the detective had gotten wrong. The door had been unlocked, so no need for tampering, and it had rained.

"If the intruders parked and walked on the pavement," she offered, "that would explain the lack of any sort of footprints or tire prints after the rain."

"It would, yes," Chance agreed. "Let's go back to when

you first arrived. Your statement said you arrived here before nine."

"Yes. We had our ceremony in the park. Everyone wished us well, and off we went. There was no reception. Honestly, it was a very small gathering. Maybe a dozen people besides our families. We had a basket prepared for our dinner that night."

"Like a picnic basket?"

She nodded, a smile pushing at her lips as she recalled her aunt's sweet wedding gift. "There was a shop in town—maybe it's still there, The Feed Store—that specialized in charcuterie boards and picnic baskets. Breads, deli meats, cheeses, fruit. That sort of thing."

"When did you bring the basket in?"

"What?" She frowned. Hadn't she mentioned that already?

"You said you went to the car for your bags, but you didn't mention the basket or the champagne."

Think, Rory! They had packed the SUV and then hurried to the park. She had dressed in the back seat after Pete walked out to join those waiting for their arrival. She'd already had her dress on before she remembered her shoes were in the cargo area. She'd had to hike up the skirt of her dress to get in the proper position to reach back there and find her shoes amid their two overnight bags.

The basket wasn't in the vehicle. Then she remembered… Austin was bringing the basket and the champagne to the cottage ahead of their arrival.

"The basket and the champagne were already here." Mystery solved.

"Who brought them?"

"My brother. Austin."

"So he had a key?"

"No. The lock on the door then was the same as the one now."

"A smart lock," he said. "You gave him the code?"

"Yes." How had she forgotten about that? In all fairness, what happened that night had obliterated most other thoughts and memories around that time frame. No one had ever asked about the food basket or the champagne. She supposed it hadn't been relevant.

"But the police didn't find his prints?"

The question jarred her. "No…they said only mine and Pete's prints were found." That had to be wrong. She looked to Chance. "How can that be?"

"It can't. Not if they actually did their job."

Wow. The investigation had gotten at least three things wrong, it seemed. As her aunt would have said, the third time was the charm.

The reality had anticipation searing through her. "It's true, then. They didn't even try to find anyone else. They barely bothered with an investigation at all."

"I'm a firm supporter of the police and what they do. But it's sounding that way to this detective." He glanced around the room. "I'd like you to walk around. Touch things. Furniture…the wall…a doorknob. Take your time. Focus on where you are and the sensation of touching each place, each item. Think of having seen or touched it that night."

Rory stood. She walked into the kitchen area first. Allowed her hand to glide along the crisp white countertop. She tugged at a drawer pull. Walked to the French doors that provided yet another view of the lake. She traced the ornate antique brass handle. Closed her hand around it. She felt warm and happy. Excited.

Even a weekend getaway at this charming little cottage had felt wonderful because she had just become Mrs. Peter Harris. She remembered they had made a toast on the balcony outside these doors. The moonlight had shimmered on the water.

She wandered away from the view and back toward the bedroom. As she passed the dining table, she allowed her fingers to glide along that surface too. Flickers of memories flashed frantically in her mind. Her body stretched out on one end of the table. Pete making love to her. She passed through the bedroom door, touched the knob there. Allowed her fingers to slide across the soft white bed linens and fluffy stack of pillows.

Pete's deep voice rumbled in the back of her mind, teasing the places his lips had touched…her ear, her neck. Their soft laughter. The sound of their kisses…of their bodies coming together. The sweet memories tugged at her heart.

Then the shouted words… Pete's voice. The disturbance had woken her from a dead sleep. She had thrown back the covers and dropped her feet to the cool wood floor. The shouting grew louder. She'd hurried to the bedroom door.

Then…

Emotion clogging her throat, Rory turned around.

Chance stood in the doorway.

The gasp escaped before she could stop it. She pressed the fingers of her right hand to her mouth. Her heart battered her breastbone so hard she couldn't catch a breath.

"Sorry. I didn't mean to sneak up on you. You didn't answer me, so I came to see if you'd found or remembered something."

She pointed to him, tears burning her eyes. "He was right there…in the door just like you are now."

"Pete?"

"No. The man in the mask." She pressed her lips together to hold back a sob. "The…the one who…raped me."

She fell against Chance's broad shoulder and let the tears flow. He whispered assurances that she was safe now. Slowly she calmed and started to voice the horrific memory.

"All I could see were his eyes and his lips. He stared at me for a moment, and then he smiled." She shuddered. "I shouted for Pete, but the other room had gone silent."

Chance didn't let go until the tears subsided. She drew back, swiped at her cheeks. "I'm sorry. The memory was just so intense. It was like I was back there, and then when I turned around and you were standing right where he had been, it was so vivid."

He took her hand and led her back to the sofa. When she'd settled, he resumed his seat. "In your statement, you said the intruder pulled you from the bed."

She gave a succinct nod, then shook her head. "No. That was wrong. His voice—I suppose it was his voice— pulled me from the bed. The shouting. I heard Pete, and I heard someone else. Shouting. Arguing. I got up to come see what was happening, and the intruder was suddenly there in the doorway just as you were a moment ago. He grabbed me and threw me back onto the bed. I fought him, but he was too strong. All I could see were his eyes… brown, not so dark like yours but brown for sure. He… you know what he did next."

Chance nodded, his expression somber. "Did you hear the voices in this room again during or after the attack?"

"No." She tilted her head and replayed those moments again. "It was all quiet. Just the sound of his…grunting." She shuddered.

"What do you remember next?"

"I suddenly broke through the fear that had held me frozen. I remember fighting the man…screaming. I bit him…scratched him." Her pulse raced faster with each remembered action. "I remember a stab in my shoulder." She frowned. "But it couldn't have been the man on top of me because his hands were on me at that point. One on my mouth…the other grasping my hair."

"His partner must have come in and drugged you. He'd probably already done the same to Pete."

A blade of pain speared through her. "I guess so. But it was sudden," she said, thinking about how she heard the shouting and then abruptly it was all quiet. "I mean, it was seconds. Not a whole minute." She looked to the man asking the questions. "They said there was no tissue under my fingernails, but that can't be right. I know I had to have scratched him."

"Your fingernails may have been cleaned after you were unconscious. A professional would know all the things to do to clean up after himself."

Something, a memory, either real or imagined, flickered through her…a gloved hand holding her hand. Had her hands and beneath her fingernails been cleaned? If not, the evidence that might have been there had been ignored. But there was no way to prove any such thing.

"You mentioned that you dream about that night."

She nodded. "All the time." She searched his face. Appreciated that his expression was thoughtful, seemed caring. Other than her aunt and her brother, it had been a long time since anyone showed her those considerations.

"Can you tell me what the dreams are about? Specifically?"

Rory drew in a deep breath. "In one of the dreams, it's

like the man who…attacked me was nervous." She shook her head. "I'm sorry. I know that sounds crazy, but I felt him tremble. But in that moment, what it meant didn't register. Or even that it happened. So I'm not sure if that part is real or not. It feels like it was—in the dreams, I mean."

"It may have been the adrenaline," he offered. "Different people have different physical reactions to pleasure as well as danger. Are there other ones? Different dreams? Different details? Conflicting or otherwise?"

"In one dream, I can feel myself being lifted and carried. The next thing I know, I'm lying on the floor with Pete. My arm goes across his body, but I didn't move it. It's as if someone else put it there. I could see Pete, and I was aware of what was happening, but I couldn't react."

"Did you recognize either intruder's voice?" he asked then.

She recalled the sounds…her frantic efforts to defend herself. The heated words from the man attacking her… or were they from the other man? She shook her head. "Their voices were odd. It's like they exaggerated the sounds when they spoke. Growled or spoke through their teeth, whatever, to ensure they weren't recognizable. But really, they didn't speak much at all. When they did, it was not in normal tones."

"You said the two of you drank the champagne. Did you eat any of the food? Do you remember having anything out on the table or on the counter? Where was the basket when you called it a night?"

She thought about that one for a bit. "I don't remember eating. Maybe that's why the champagne went to my head, and my memory is foggier than it should have been."

"So you never touched any of the eating utensils or knives in the kitchen."

"No. I never even opened the fridge." Heat rose in her cheeks. "We just went straight to the bedroom when we arrived. We went out on the balcony once. Pete had the glasses and the bottle of champagne. At one point we were at the table, but there was nothing on it. No basket, no food." She concentrated harder on the details. "I'm fairly certain I didn't touch much of anything beyond furniture."

"In the one hundred and thirty two crime scene photos," he said, his gaze steady on hers, "all the things you said were in the basket were spread on the table. There were plates and glasses. They gave the appearance that the two of you had been at the table eating."

That wasn't right. "No. I'm certain we never used the table. Not for eating."

"Someone did. There were half-eaten portions of bread and cheese. Bare grape stems. Either someone ate, or they went to great lengths to make it look as if the two of you had eaten."

"Detective Fowler never mentioned anything about the food or the table." She looked at the table. "But if we didn't eat, that would mean…"

Dear God, she couldn't even say the words.

"It would imply that the men," Chance said for her, "who murdered your husband and attacked you ate before they left or prepared the table as if someone had eaten."

Chapter Six

White Cottage
Scenic Drive
Hollywood, 10:00 a.m.

Rory stopped to have a last look at the cottage before getting back into the car. The hurt swelled inside her all over again. How was it possible that the tragedy of that night had been over two years ago and the truth about who killed her husband still had not been found? Was no one doing their job in all this time?

"Rory."

She looked across the hood at Chance who had spoken just as a car door slammed. Her attention swung to the street, as did his.

The ostentatious sedan that sat on the otherwise empty street was one Rory recognized well. But it was the woman who had emerged from the vehicle that sent dread spreading through her.

Eudora Harris. Pete's mother.

Blond hair expertly twisted into a bun, form-fitting peach-colored sheath showing off her youthful figure, Eudora stood at the end of the driveway, effectively blocking their path.

"How dare you come here," the woman snarled as she took a few steps in their direction. "You should be ashamed of yourself."

"Hello, Eudora." Rory braced for her former mother-in-law's anger. This would not be pleasant. Not that she blamed the woman. She thought Rory killed her son—her only child. Of course she would spew vitriol at the sight of her. Still, Rory had other reasons to despise the woman.

Eudora glanced at Chance then. "I heard you had hired some private detective to try and confirm your lies." Her attention swung back to Rory, her face twisted with fury and hatred. "Why waste your time? You know what you did. We all know what you did. You're wasting your time and the taxpayers' dollars by resurrecting this investigation. Scottsboro doesn't need to see a rehash of that nightmare. I—" she slapped a hand against her chest "—do not want you or your minion here."

Rory wished there had been a time when she felt something for this woman, but Eudora had made sure that never happened. She had disliked Rory from the beginning. The only thing they ever shared was love for Pete. Well, and grief after his death. This behavior from her was not surprising. Rory had expected Pete's parents to still hate her, maybe even more than ever after the conviction was overturned.

"My agency rented this cottage for the week, Mrs. Harris," Chance said.

His words had no effect on the woman. She remained standing at the end of the driveway, arms crossed over her chest, and staring at Rory. "You need to leave this town," she warned. "You are not welcome here. Whatever you believe you can prove with your lies is never going to happen. You will go back to prison where you belong."

Anger kindled deep in Rory's belly despite her best attempts to tamp it down. She stepped away from the car. Started toward the older woman. She didn't look back, but she sensed Chance had followed her. "I'm sorry you lost your son," Rory told her. "But I lost my husband. You should be glad the police are looking into the investigation again, because the persons who killed him got away with it. Don't you care that they're out there, living their lives as if they did nothing wrong?"

Eudora laughed. "There you go again, trying to pretend innocence. You killed him." Her gaze narrowed; her face hardened. "And whatever it takes for however long it takes, I will make sure you spend the rest of your life in prison."

With that, she did an about-face and stormed back to her extravagant car. She climbed in and sped away.

"So that was the matriarch of the family," Chance said as her car faded in the distance.

"That was her." Rory felt suddenly tired. "She hated me from day one. She and her husband were certain Pete was too good for me. I had no business intruding in his life. But the truth was, he intruded in mine."

Chance put his hand at the small of her back and ushered her to the passenger side of his rental car. "How so?"

Rory reached for the door handle but hesitated before opening it. She smiled. "He saw me at the school. He had attended Caldwell as a kid. He and his family are big donors to the schools. He served as the MC at one of our staff events. From that night until the night he was murdered, he saw me or called me every day. Every single day." She gave her head a shake. "I tried to ignore him at first. I was dating someone else, and in truth, I could not imagine what a Harris would want to do with me. He was the most eligible bachelor in the county. He could have anyone he wanted."

Chance leaned against the car, his eyes searching hers. "But he wanted you."

She laughed softly. "Apparently. And there was something about him…something that I couldn't resist. So I decided to see where things went. You know the rest."

Rory opened the door and got into the car. Chance readied to close it but paused. "You do not give yourself nearly enough credit, Aurora Harris."

She laughed, a weary sound. "Thanks."

He closed the door and rounded the hood. Though she appreciated the compliment, it was difficult to feel good about herself anymore. There was a time when she was proud of her work, proud of what she had accomplished. But all that ended on her wedding night. Add all those nights in prison and she felt worthless most of the time.

She was reasonably confident she would never look at herself with any sort of pride again. Not here for sure. As Eudora said, Rory could never have a life here again. To pretend otherwise was foolish. Didn't matter anyway. If the detective and the district attorney had their way, she would be going back to prison. She imagined the Harrises were donating heavily to the cause.

Rory thought of the friends of Pete's who had broken her window. And the other two who had vandalized her home. They all thought she was a murderer. Of course they didn't want her back in town. She could just imagine what today's headlines would look like. Some hungry reporter would have heard about her return already.

No matter. Rory was back in Scottsboro. Whether she stayed was irrelevant. The one thing that mattered was finding the truth and making sure the persons who murdered her husband were brought to justice.

She glanced at the man who settled behind the steering wheel. He would help make that happen. If she'd had any doubt whatsoever, she had none now. Just this morning, he had helped her to see several holes in the first investigation. Whether the detective was incompetent or had some other agenda, he had ignored those details.

There would be no ignoring them now.

Kindred Residence
Tupelo Pike
Scottsboro, 11:30 a.m.

RORY HAD CALLED her attorney's office on the way back from the cottage. She was supposed to call the attorney as soon as she was settled but she'd been a little preoccupied. She left a message with his secretary along with her new number. Hopefully he would call soon. She had a good amount to share with him already.

As Chance slowed to turn into her driveway, Rory leaned forward. Where were all the red splotches?

"Do you recognize that truck?" Chance asked.

Her gaze shifted from the house to the driveway. The tan-colored truck parked there was not one she recognized. Squinting her eyes, she studied the driver. Male. Dark hair. Cut short. His back was turned, so she couldn't see his face. He wore jeans and a checked shirt. He stood in her front yard, coiling up a water hose. She and Chance had just stopped by the hardware store and picked up a hose and a long-handled scrub brush.

Apparently they weren't going to need either now.

The man standing in her yard turned as gravel crunched under their tires.

Shane. Rory drew back, glanced at the driver. "It's Shane Carter. He's the deputy who stopped by yesterday right after I arrived. He's Pete's cousin."

"Looks like he did our work for us." Chance shut off the engine.

Shane waved, and Rory reached for her door. Maybe there was one person in this town who didn't hate her. "I'm grateful. After that run-in with Pete's mom, it's nice to have someone at least act like a friend."

Chance agreed, "A helping hand is always appreciated."

They emerged from the vehicle. Chance tagged along behind her since Shane was someone she knew. Rory worked up a smile for the man. "Wow. That was sure a nice surprise to come home to."

Shane shook his head. "It's a disgrace. I heard about it at the station early this morning. I came by, but you were gone." He shrugged. "I figured you wouldn't mind me taking care of the mess." His attention settled on Chance then. He gave him a nod of acknowledgment.

"I'm sorry." Rory gestured to the man now standing at her side. "This is Chance Rader. He's a private investigator helping me in my search for the truth."

"Good to meet you." Shane extended his hand.

Chance gave his hand a shake. "Same." He glanced at the house. "It was good of you to take care of this."

"No problem, man, really." Shane's expression turned somber. "It's a damned shame you have to go through this again, Rory. I want you to know I'm doing all I can to help. I'm asking questions and digging around. If I find or learn anything, I'll be sure to let you know."

Rory would never find the right words to adequately

articulate how much she appreciated the effort. "We can use all the help we can get. I think you're the only person in the county who believes me."

"Anyone who really knows you," Shane countered, "should know you couldn't possibly have hurt Pete. It's bull."

"I just hope I can prove it," Rory granted. What else was there to say? Now the burden of proof was back on her. She knew better than to trust the system that supposedly presumed a person was innocent until proven guilty. It had already failed her once. She wasn't repeating that mistake again.

"Were you close to Pete?" Chance asked Shane.

Shane shifted his attention to him once more. "Sure. We were cousins. I knew him my whole life. Family reunions. Holidays. He was a year older than me and big into sports, so we didn't really hang out a lot, you know. But we were there for each other."

"Did you ever have any disagreements with him or his parents?"

Shane looked taken aback by the question. "What is that supposed to mean?"

Rory wasn't sure if she should say something to reassure Shane. Chance was the expert here. She certainly didn't want to get in the way of his investigation, no matter that she felt certain he was asking the wrong person such a pointed question.

"It doesn't mean anything," Chance said. "I'll ask everyone we talk to that same question. Sometimes even the little things from the past can make a difference. Any sort of disagreement can shed light on Pete's thinking in a given situation. Perhaps provide some insight not yet considered."

"No," Shane said, his tone cross, impatient. "Pete and I never had any issues. Ever. He was a good guy. So are his parents. They do a lot for the community. Pete did as well. He had no enemies that I know of. Everybody liked him."

"And yet," Chance countered, "he was murdered."

This time Rory felt taken aback by his comment. Before she could say anything, Shane stepped forward, going toe to toe with Chance.

"It had to be a random act of violence," Shane argued. "No one who knew Pete would have wanted him dead."

Chance held his ground. "Why not break into the home Pete and Rory shared? There were far more options for taking sellable goods. There was pretty much nothing at that cottage. In fact, the only things the intruders took were cell phones. Petty stuff. You're a cop. Why do you suppose that is?"

"You'd have to ask Detective Fowler. I had no part in the investigation." Shane backed off a step, shifted his attention to Rory. "If I had been involved, I would have made sure things turned out differently."

"How?" Chance asked, drawing his gaze back to him.

"What?" Shane snapped.

Rory looked from one to the other. The conversation had quickly escalated to an uncomfortable level. She fully expected one or both to start throwing punches. "Shane, I don't think—"

"How," Chance repeated, "would you have conducted the investigation any differently? I'd really like to hear what you mean. If you believe Fowler failed to do his duty, any information you can offer to help Rory would be genuinely appreciated."

Shane's jaw worked as if he struggled to find the right

words. Finally, he snapped, "I think Fowler ignored evidence."

Rory bit back a gasp. She had fully believed this from the beginning, but this was the first time she had heard anyone say the words. That it was someone—even a friend and relative of Pete's—involved in law enforcement shocked her.

"What evidence, specifically?" Chance shot back. "Beyond the part he failed to share, which cost him the first conviction."

When Shane hesitated, Rory urged, "Please. If you have information that will help me, please tell us."

"I can't prove anything," he said with a covert glance around. "But there were rumors that Fowler was getting pressure to close the case. To make sure you didn't get away with what you'd done."

"Who would do such a thing?" Rory felt sick at the idea that someone with enough power to pressure the detective in charge of her case had done this. She just didn't understand why. She had never harmed anyone in this town. The answer had to be one or both of his parents. Not that she had ever done a single thing to them—other than to marry their son.

"His mother," Shane confessed, falling back another step as if he'd been pushed. "But you can't tell anyone I told you this." He looked from Rory to Chance and back. "I'm serious. She wants you to spend the rest of your life in prison. She will take down anyone in her way."

Rory shouldn't really be surprised but hearing it confirmed was difficult. Eudora had never liked her. Not that Rory had ever harmed or wronged her in any way. But she hadn't been good enough for her son. Just a poor girl from the wrong side of the tracks, literally.

"But what evidence did Fowler ignore?" Chance pressed. "It's a broad statement that by itself won't help Rory. We need something to go on—a place to start."

Shane held up his hands in a gesture of surrender. "Okay, I'll admit I don't have anything specific that will help except the rumors and the knowledge that you couldn't have done this. I know you couldn't have."

Rory's hopes wilted. "Why didn't you come forward during the investigation? You could have told me or my attorney what you were hearing. You could have vouched for me." Austin and Lulu were the only people who spoke for her.

"I was between a rock and a hard place, Rory." He shook his head, his shoulders slumped in defeat. "I had just been notified I got on with the sheriff's department. I couldn't screw that up. Especially since all I had were rumors, and most of those I didn't hear until it was too late."

"Thank you for telling me, but I need to get inside." She felt sick. Every time she dared to get her hopes up, she had the rug pulled out from under her all over again.

"Wait." Shane touched her arm. "Give me a chance, Rory. I promise I won't let you down this time. I won't sit on the sidelines and ignore what's happening. I swear."

Chance stepped between them. "Thanks for taking care of the house, but you should go now."

Shane dropped his hand and headed back over to where he'd left the cleanup tools.

Rory couldn't let him leave this way. "Shane, I'm sorry."

His head came up, and he stared at her hopefully, like a misbehaving puppy who had just been given a second opportunity to do better.

"If you really want to help," she said, hoping Chance

wouldn't mind her taking this initiative, "find something that will help us prove the truth. We need evidence. Our word alone—yours and mine—won't be enough. We already know how this will go if I don't find evidence. Or figure out how the one piece of this they left out fits. I need a witness or something."

The water hose in hand, Shane rejoined them on the driveway. "I swear to you," he looked from Rory to Chance, "and you, that I will do everything in my power to find whatever I can. I want to help. You have no idea how much I want to help. I failed you and I failed Pete last time. It's weighed on me every day for the past two years."

"Thank you, Shane," Rory said, drumming up a smile. "I will be forever in your debt if you do."

His smile widened. "I won't let you down. I promise."

He gave Chance a nod and headed for his truck. He tossed the coiled up hose in the back and climbed in. When he'd driven away, Chance asked, "Do you think he means what he says?"

Rory wished she knew the answer. "I hope so. I really, really hope so."

"You have every reason not to trust him," Chance reminded her.

He was right. She laughed. "Like I said, I can't trust right now, but I can hope."

He smiled then, and she felt buoyed by it. Such a nice smile. Having someone on her side was a good feeling. One she hadn't felt beyond her little family in a long time.

"You can," he agreed. "But I think we can do better than just hope. We already know of at least four places where Fowler fell down on the job. We're going to fill in those missing pieces, and then we'll prove what he ignored and find the truth about what really happened that night."

Chance was right. They could do better than just hoping. Rory damned well intended to prove her innocence. She thought of Eudora Harris. No matter what the woman believed, Rory would make her see that she was wrong.

They were all wrong.

Chapter Seven

Kindred Residence
Tupelo Pike
Scottsboro, 12:00 p.m.

Rory removed the cheese and butter from the fridge. "We could have grilled cheese sandwiches."

"Works for me." Chance reached for the loaf of bread on the counter.

"Mayo?" she asked before closing the fridge door.

"None for me."

She smiled. "Me either. The cheese is the best part of a grilled cheese. Why dilute it with anything else?"

He held up a finger. "Except pickles. On the side, of course."

"Pickles." She made a face as she tried to think if she'd noticed any. "I hope I have pickles. Check the cabinets, and I'll get the sandwiches started."

Rory reached into the drawer under the oven and retrieved her aunt's favorite cast iron skillet. She placed it on top and dug for the matches in the cabinet drawer next to the stove. The appliance was vintage—as in many decades old. Her aunt had loved it. She'd found it at an auction about forty years ago. With the help of her boyfriend at the time, she had completely restored it. The bright yellow color was so Lulu. The important part for Rory was that it worked. The downside was it ran on gas and required manual lighting. The poof that happened when she set the flame to the burner always made her jump.

The instant heat meant the butter melted and started to sizzle quickly. She placed two slices of cheese between two pieces of bread and added them to the pan. A quick turn ensured both sides got a little of that melted butter. Extra cheese was the key, in her opinion, to the best grilled cheese sandwiches.

"Ah-ha," Chance announced. "We have pickles." He placed the jar on the counter.

"Better check the date." Rory laughed. "Just in case."

Chance rolled the jar around in his hand, inspecting the glass as well as the label. He swiped the dust off the top against his shirt. "We're good." He sat the jar aside. "What else can I do?"

"Grab a plate." She gestured to the plate rack above the sink. "Grab two, actually."

When the plates were on the counter, Rory slid the first sandwich onto one, then quickly added more butter to the skillet and prepped the next one. Chance opened the pickle jar and added slices to each plate.

With the second sandwich done and the stove turned off, Rory sliced the two diagonally across the middle the way her aunt had always done. "We are ready," she announced.

Chance was at the fridge. He held up bottles of water. "You good with water?"

"Absolutely."

They settled at the table and focused on their sandwiches for a while. There was a lot they needed to talk about, but eating took priority. Plus, it was good to have a few minutes to consider the events of the morning before starting the discussion about what they meant. Rory was still struggling to gain her footing after the encounter with Eudora Harris. The idea that she was the mother of the man Rory had loved with all her heart was not only painful but disappointing. How could she have had so little confidence in her son? Pete was a good, intelligent man. He wouldn't have been fooled by anyone.

But the ugly events of last night and this morning were precisely why when she first learned the news that a technicality might well give her a second chance at corroborating her innocence, she hadn't been as excited about it as she should have been. She had really doubted that it would ever happen. Pete's parents would see to it that she never had an opportunity for leaving that prison. After all, the find wasn't that big or even particularly important, as best she could determine. A technician at the lab where all the evidence had been sent had gotten in touch with her attorney's clerk and admitted that a single piece of evidence tested had not made its way into court. The DA's office had claimed the evidence was irrelevant. An anomaly that was insufficient to change the course of the trial. And maybe it was—unaccounted-for fibers could be nothing, but they were on her body and on Pete's, and that tiny, minute bit of fibers had not been found anywhere at the crime scene or in their shared home or in either of their vehicles. It truly was an anomaly that presented the opportunity to suggest someone else had been at the scene. That someone other than her had committed murder.

The DA had insisted it was insufficient to suggest someone else was the murderer.

By the same token, so was the evidence that she had

committed murder. There really was no direct physical evidence beyond her presence at the scene and her prints on the murder weapon.

Okay, so maybe her prints being on the murder weapon was stronger.

Weeks after this revelation, the news came that she was being released. Even then she had decided it had to be a mistake. That someone would stop the process before she could get outside the walls of that awful place. Each night she would go to sleep convinced that the next day she would be told it was all an error…a misunderstanding.

It wasn't until she was outside the gate that she acknowledged it was actually happening. It was real.

She finished her sandwich and wiped her hands on the paper towel in her lap. She wanted to ask so many things but wasn't sure how to begin. Instead, she reached for her water and sipped it until Chance kicked off the discussion. He had finished his sandwich and was looking at something on his cell phone. She had no idea if it was about her case or a text from his girlfriend or wife. She realized then that other than his professional credentials, she really knew nothing about him.

Except that he was kind. Patient. Caring. And good at this job.

He looked up as if she'd said the words aloud. "You made the headlines of the local paper." He turned the screen around for her to see.

There was her face all right—a photo from her days as a teacher—on the screen beneath the headline, *The Murder Bride Is Back for Round Two*. Nothing she hadn't expected. "Oh yay."

He smiled. "It sells papers." He glanced at the screen once more. "Nice pic."

She scoffed. "I'm just glad they didn't use one from my wedding the way they did last time." She shuddered. It had felt like a stab to her heart to see the photo of her and Pete from that beautiful day turned into something so malicious as the story of how it appeared she had murdered him in cold blood.

Chance laid his phone aside. "Tell me about Shane Carter."

Rory thought about this for a moment. "He grew up here, and so did I. He was related to Pete, so of course I knew who he was. I think I saw him at one of their family reunions once." She frowned. "Wait, no. It was a birthday party for Anthony, Pete's father. Anyway, Shane was always nice to me."

"So you don't really *know* him," Chance suggested. "You're not familiar with his friends, his love life or anything actually personal."

She nodded. "That's right. I have no idea who his other friends are or were. I honestly don't recall ever seeing him with anyone I assumed to be a girlfriend. I had no idea he'd applied for a position with the Jackson County Sheriff's Department." She made a face. "I guess I really don't know him much at all. But I do recall that at that birthday party, he stayed on the fringes." She shrugged. "Like he wasn't really part of things. At the time I felt a sort of kinship with him. Like we were both outsiders… not really part of the family."

"He comes off as a nice guy," Chance suggested. He picked up his water bottle, downed a sip. "Concerned. Helpful. But very nonspecific about it all."

She nodded, seeing his point immediately. "He didn't really tell us anything, just alluded to *things*."

Chance braced his forearms on the table and leaned

forward. "I got the feeling he knows more than he's sharing. Maybe it's the job stopping him from saying more, maybe it's the family, but something or someone is holding him back."

Anticipation fired in Rory's veins. They so desperately needed some discovery to help in moving forward with their investigation. "He might actually know what evidence was overlooked but is afraid to share it since the family would disown him and his job might come into question."

"He was just starting with the sheriff's department when Pete was murdered."

Rory nodded. "He didn't want to make waves—he said as much. It was either help me or hang on to the job." Wow, now that she said the words out loud, it was disheartening to realize that her life was not as important as someone's job—someone who was supposed to be a friend. Pete's own cousin.

"Then again," Chance said, "he probably recognized given the power and influence of the Harris family that he would be fighting an uphill battle. Whatever he did or said might not have changed anything other than his job offer."

There was that. "But has that probability changed? If he helps me now, his job may still be in jeopardy. I'm sure the family would ostracize him. Basically, he's facing the same potential losses now that he did then. So why speak up now?"

"Which could possibly mean he sees things differently now," Chance offered. "Or he sees an opportunity that he didn't see then."

Rory wasn't sure she understood. A frown lined her brow, emphasizing the distant ache that had started there. She really hadn't slept well last night. The vandals combined with the fact that a stranger, basically, was in the house with her made staying asleep difficult. She considered the man seated on the other side of the table. Admittedly, he didn't feel like a stranger…but he was, and maybe on some level her mind had become obsessed with that fact, not allowing her to sleep deeply enough.

She asked, "What sort of opportunity do you mean?"

"He has time and experience in the department now. What better way to achieve that next step up the career ladder than to bust open a big case? This is a big case, Rory. It stayed in the headlines for a long time even after you were sentenced. It's already back in the headlines now, and the new trial date hasn't even been set. He could right a grievous mistake, which makes for even bigger headlines. There are plenty of people who like to see the underdog win. The Harris power element may not carry the same weight it did before."

She saw where he was coming from, but for the most part, the scenario wasn't a pleasant one. All it did was confirm the idea that she couldn't trust anyone beyond her brother and this man—a virtual stranger. How sad was that? Yes, it would be great if at least part of the community got behind her…but could she really count on that?

"I realize it's not something you want to hear," he went on. "But it's important that we carefully analyze all aspects of the case, including the people around you, then and now. We have to understand more than what they're telling us—assuming they tell us anything. The motive for their actions is equally important."

"The search for hidden agendas," she agreed with a shake of her head. "Whatever happened to people saying what they actually felt? Or, better yet, just telling the truth."

"Sadly," Chance warned, "it's no longer that simple."

He was right. Nothing was, she admitted silently.

"Let's talk about your former mother-in-law."

Rory laughed. "She always disliked me. Always. Before I was involved with her son, I was just a nuisance to be tolerated."

"The two of you had some sort of relationship prior to your meeting Pete?" The possibility appeared to surprise him.

It was a small town. Everyone knew everyone else. "Not really a relationship." Rory thought about how to explain the situation. "The Harris family donates heavily to the local schools. Really, they give a tremendous amount of support, and I wouldn't want to in any way belittle what they do when it comes to community support." She thought back to the early days of teaching. "I obviously knew of the family, but I didn't *know* the family. When I was selected as teacher of the year, that changed really fast."

"How so?"

"Eudora is the one who bestows that honor each year. We met for the first time at the annual gathering where the awards are given." Thinking back, Rory had to shake her head. "After my name was announced and I walked up to the podium—while we waited for the applause to settle—she said in an aside that I shouldn't let it go to my head. I later learned that it was expected for a new, young teacher to receive the award every other year. It was a self-esteem boost. There are never enough teachers, and extra incentives are always a good thing. But Eudora went a step further. She suggested that it was always the prettiest one who was chosen—leaving me to believe it wasn't about merit."

"Seriously?"

Rory rolled her eyes. "Seriously."

"It would be interesting to know if she said something similar to past award winners." He made a distasteful face. "Wow."

"Yeah," Rory agreed. "No matter what she said, I know several past winners, and I have to say, they really are outstanding teachers. I honestly believe she just didn't like me for whatever reason, and she wanted to make sure the award didn't go to my head."

"How long after that before you met Pete?"

"It was the next school term. Seven months." She laughed then. "The first time he took me to dinner at their home was tense. He'd told his parents that he'd met someone, but he didn't say who. When we arrived, it was very obvious that Eudora had gone all-out. She wanted to impress Pete's new girlfriend. When she saw that it was me, well, let's just say she was startled. She was discombobulated the entire evening. His father remained oddly quiet. When he drove me home, Pete apologized repeatedly for their odd behavior. He kept saying he wasn't sure why they were acting so strangely. But I knew."

"Did you ever tell him about her remark when you received the award?"

"No. She was his mother. I didn't want to be that person—you know, the girlfriend who rats out her soon-to-be mother-in-law."

"I'm guessing she wasn't so nice about her own feelings."

"Oh. No." Rory shuddered at the memories. "She called me the next day after that dinner and asked me to lunch. We'd barely sat down when she proceeded to tell me all the reasons I was not fit to be her son's girlfriend."

Chance leaned back in his chair, his expression puzzled. "She just out and said it, did she?"

"Eudora is not one to mince words. She was very frank. Her son had a bright future that she insisted involved great wealth and enormous power, including political influence. He would be moving up in the world, and the woman at his side was immensely important to his image. I did not fit that image in any shape, form or fashion."

His eyebrows reared up. "I'm sure you had to tell Pete about this."

Again, Rory shook her head. "No. I talked to Aunt Lulu about it. She suggested I keep quiet and allow Eudora enough rope to hang herself. I wasn't happy about the idea at first, but as it turned out, Lulu was right. The more I ignored Eudora's warnings, the harder she tried to thwart our relationship. The more she tried, the more obvious she became. Even Pete had started to notice. The last straw was only a week before our wedding when she offered her son an exorbitant sum of money to dump me and move on. Pete was infuriated. She walked back the offer, of course. Insisting that she was only trying to protect him since she'd learned some very bad things about me."

A frown furrowed Chance's forehead. "What sort of bad things?"

"Lies, of course. She paid some guy I had never met to claim we'd had an affair and that he would release compromising photos of me if I didn't pay him. I had never met the guy much less been in a compromising position with him."

"How did the two of you handle it?"

She shrugged. "I don't know how it went down, but Pete handled it. He told me not to worry. It wouldn't happen again."

"Do you recall the man's name?"

"Taylor Banks. Everyone called him Tay. He was only a couple of years older than me. Back then he was a known sleazebag. I don't know about these days. But at the time, he lived with his mother over on Houston Street." Rory shrugged. "He was one of those guys who would do most anything for money. And if asked, he claimed to be experienced in all things." She laughed. "If someone was in need of a mechanic, he would swear he'd worked on cars his whole life when he had no clue how to check the oil, much less determine the cause of a malfunction."

Chance picked up his phone. "Let's see if we can figure out what he's up to now."

Rory could just imagine. The man was a swindler of the highest order.

"Looks like," Chance said, studying the screen, "Mr. Banks still lives on Houston Street." His attention shifted to her. "I'll send his name and address to the agency. See if they can pull up a criminal record or anything of interest."

"It might not be a bad idea to see if he's willing to talk about the deal he and Eudora made." She turned her hands up. "I suppose he might have an in with the local scumbag grapevine. He may have even heard things about what really happened to Pete." Hurt swelled in her chest. The idea that someone knew the truth and hadn't come forward made her feel ill.

"As soon as I hear back from my contact at the agency, we'll do that. For now, let's consider a different avenue. Were you ever aware of anyone who might have been envious of Pete? Had a grudge of some sort against him? Or maybe just wanted to see him fall from his high position in the community?"

She frowned. "I don't think Pete had any enemies. Everyone liked him." She smiled. "I know sometimes people say that and it's an exaggeration, but really, I never met or heard of anyone who didn't like him."

Chance held her gaze but said nothing.

It took a moment, but she suddenly understood the mistake she had made. Yes, she had met someone who didn't like him. Two someones, in fact. The night he was murdered, those two intruders had tortured him, then murdered him. Was it possible that it wasn't a random act where the two thought they were in for a big score and found nothing?

She moistened her lips, wished her throat didn't suddenly feel so dry and that her eyes weren't burning as if a match had been lit there. "Sorry. I wasn't thinking. What I should have said was that beyond those two intruders, I never met anyone who didn't like Pete or who wanted to hurt him."

Chance reached across the table and took her hand in his. "You see, that's the problem we have. There are people who are envious of others. People who feel slighted by some deal that perhaps was a really good deal for all involved except that one person. Scarier than either of those options are the people who've known you your whole life and have wished you harm—for whatever reason—from afar. When that person crosses the line, it's always the worst-case scenario."

She reminded herself to breathe. "You're saying that the person responsible for what happened could be someone he knew well. Maybe someone he worked with. Or was related to." A tear escaped her harsh hold. She swiped viciously at it with her free hand.

He nodded. "That's what I'm saying. Bottom line, we can't rule anyone out. We can't assume anything. We have to operate under the theory that his own mother could have hired those intruders."

A dry laugh burst out of her then. "Well, if she did, Pete was not the target. The target was me."

"I think—" he leaned closer, took her other hand "—maybe you might be more right than you realize."

Chapter Eight

Banks Residence
North Houston Street
Scottsboro, 3:00 p.m.

Chance parked on the street in front of the small bungalow. The property needed considerable maintenance. Two cars in various stages of disassembly sat in the yard. A blue tarp on the roof suggested a leak waiting for repair. The considerable litter on the porch and banked around the foundation of the house declared the owner either wasn't capable of cleanup or lacked the desire to get the job done.

If Taylor Banks was as muscled up and physically capable these days as he had appeared in his last arrest photos, then the man should take care of the place. Sadly, his rap sheet alone implied he wasn't one to care about anything other than his next hit of whatever illegal drug he preferred on a given day.

"Why don't I go to the door first?" Chance offered. "If the guy is open to an interview, we can both go inside."

Rory looked from the run-down property to him. "Don't worry about me. The house my parents owned was just a couple of streets over. I'm familiar with the neighborhood, if that has you concerned."

Chance nodded. "We go together then."

Before he could say more, she opened her door and got out. Chance did the same. He rounded the hood and joined her on the sidewalk that led from the street to the front porch. He took his time, surveyed the block. There were several houses undergoing renovation along the block. He'd noticed considerable changes happening on the south end. He supposed the changes were slowly making their way in this direction.

Luckily there was no dog on the porch ready to give them a hard time. Rory stood aside, and Chance knocked on the door. As hard as he tried not to stare, her eyes drew him in every time he looked her way. The striking contrast of her black hair and pale skin would garner the attention of anyone in her vicinity. She reminded him of a fairy-tale creature found only in books.

"What?"

He blinked, realized he had been staring too long. "Sorry. I was just thinking." Rather than explain, he knocked again. The door was battered, the paint worn. Someone had or at least tried to jimmy the lock on more than one occasion.

With the lack of noise on the other side of the door and no serviceable vehicle in the drive, Mr. Banks might not be home.

Chance knocked a third time, louder this time.

"Hold on!" echoed from inside.

Their gazes met, his and Rory's. Apparently someone was home after all.

The door opened, and a man resembling the latest mug shot available on the net stood before them. His jeans and tee looked as if he'd lived in them for about a week. His hair was longer than in the mug shot and poked out around his head like a dark cloud. But the baseball bat held firmly in his right hand made the biggest statement about the man. Angry.

"Who the hell are you?" Banks demanded.

Chance removed his credentials case from his back pocket. He showed the ID to the guy. "Chance Rader, private investigator."

"Tay," Rory said. "You remember me? Rory Wilkins. I married Pete Harris."

Banks had kept his attention fixed on Chance until she spoke. Even then he spared her only a brief glance.

When he didn't respond, Rory added, "You came up with this story that you and I had an affair."

His gaze shot to her again, something like annoyance on his face. "I don't know what you're talking about."

"We're not here to cause you trouble," Chance assured him. "We just want to talk about what happened back then."

The disheveled man's gaze narrowed. "You got some kind of reward for information?"

"Tay Banks," Rory snapped, moving a step closer to him, "don't even go there."

"As a matter of fact," Chance intervened, "there is a reward."

Rory turned and stared at him, her expression less than pleased at the prospect of giving the guy anything.

"Depending on what you know," Chance went on, "the amount works on a sliding scale."

Banks hitched his head. "Well, come on in, then."

He turned and headed deeper into the house. Rory gave Chance a bewildered look before following Banks.

Chance supposed he should have mentioned that this was sometimes a necessary tactic. He would explain later, in the car, and hopefully she wouldn't be upset that he hadn't prepared her—particularly with a man like this who had wronged her so flagrantly.

Inside the house was in worse shape than the exterior. Dimly lit, cluttered. Smelled as bad as it looked. Empty beer cans and liquor bottles. Pizza boxes and fast-food leftovers cluttered most surfaces.

Banks pushed aside a pile of blankets and pillows on the sofa and gestured to the newly cleared area. "Have a seat."

Rory hesitated before taking him up on the offer. Chance suspected the number of not readily identifiable stains on the cushions were the reason for her reluctance. When she finally sat down, careful not to lean back, Chance did the same.

Banks dropped into the equally stained recliner he'd no doubt vacated to answer the door. He propped the baseball bat against his knee and reached to the side table for the only unopened can of beer among the half dozen or so scattered there. He popped the top and took a long swallow. Once he'd wiped his mouth with his forearm, he looked from Rory to Chance. "Let's get this party started. What do you want to know?"

"You tried to blackmail me," Rory said, not waiting for Chance. "You were lying, but that's not the part that matters. I need you to confirm who put you up to saying all those lies about me."

He made a disgusted sound. "You still think you're too good for me, don't ya? Even after going to prison for murder." He gave her a cold once-over. "You ain't no better than me. So don't even pretend."

Rory nodded. "I have never considered myself better than you or anyone else." When he would have protested, she held up her hands. "I'm not here to judge you, Tay. I'm just trying to find the truth. Can you help me with that?"

He turned his beer can around and around between his fingers. "I get it. You're still trying to prove you didn't kill your husband."

Evidently, Chance decided, the man didn't watch the news or he would know there was going to be a new trial. Not exactly surprising. He glanced around the room. The old box-type television probably didn't work, and even if it did, the news likely wasn't on his up-next list.

"Yes, I am," she admitted, her chin going up in protest of the way her voice trembled. "Because I didn't kill him."

"What we're looking for," Chance explained, "is any information you know firsthand or may have heard about Pete Harris's murder."

"And the identity of who put you up to blackmail me," Rory tacked on.

"First off," Banks said, his gaze fixed on Rory, "I ain't telling you nothing until I see the money."

"This is not a negotiation," Chance warned. "If the information you provide is worth hearing, then you'll be paid. Until we hear it and make that determination, we are not going there."

"Fine," he spat. He looked to Rory once more. "Anyone who ain't stupid knows you didn't kill him." He downed another long swallow of beer. "Do I know anything that can prove you didn't? I wish. But there are people who do know stuff. You can bet your sweet ass on that."

"Who hired you to try and blackmail me?" Rory repeated.

Banks grinned, laughed a little. "You should know the

answer to that, girl. She hated your guts. It's a flat-out miracle she didn't put out a·hit on you."

Rory stared at him but said nothing more. She had the answer to her question.

Chance picked up the conversation from there. "You're suggesting Eudora Harris paid you to pretend you possessed scandalous photos of Rory and that the two of you had a relationship."

He gave a single nod. "She did. Paid me five hundred dollars up front. All I had to do was say all that stuff and then not tell anyone who hired me. If I did everything just like she said, when it was all over, she'd give me another five Benjamins for keeping quiet."

"You said," Chance ventured, "there were people who knew things. Who would you go to if you wanted the facts about what happened to Pete Harris?"

A grin kicked up one side of the man's mouth. "That sounds more like advice you're looking for than just plain old information. You asking me for advice, hotshot?"

Chance nodded. "I am."

"Just so you know—" Banks leaned forward, braced his elbows on his knees "—advice costs extra."

"All right. Let's hear your advice."

"Well—" he looked from Chance to Rory and back "—first off, I wouldn't bother with his people. That family don't let nobody see or hear about their issues. Ever. So you'll never get nothing from one of them. My advice would be to go to the police."

Rory's mouth gaped. "Seriously? Is that the best you've got? The police are the ones who said it was me who killed him. Why would I go to them?"

Banks allowed his grin to widen. "Come on, girl. Think. Just cause they said it was you don't mean they didn't know it wasn't."

Chapter Nine

Kindred Residence
Tupelo Pike
Scottsboro, 6:00 p.m.

Rory had played tour guide for the past couple of hours. The memories that haunted her along the way were bittersweet. After giving that lowlife Tay Banks a hundred bucks, they had driven by the sheriff's department and police department as well as the courthouse. They had cruised around the downtown square, and she had pointed out the corner drugstore where she'd had her first job back in high school.

The tour had continued to Cumberland Court, where Pete's parents lived on the very edge of the peninsula jutting into the lake. The house was massive, far larger than they had ever needed, Rory explained, but it was stunning, isolated and flanked by water on three sides as if it were in the middle of the ocean. The home provided the ostentatious setting that suited the image and lifestyle the Harris family wanted the world to see.

By contrast, the house Rory and Pete had purchased together was on Buchannan Street, only blocks from Caldwell Elementary where she had taught third grade.

Pete could have bought any house he wanted, but he understood how very much she had wanted to live in that neighborhood. Showing off hadn't been his style despite having grown up in that mansion.

As they had driven past Rory's former home, Chance had slowed. The house looked dark and lonely, but thankfully there was no sign of vandalism. She imagined everything was just as it had been—except for her possessions, of course. Eudora had likely ensured that all signs of Rory were removed. Eventually, she supposed they would sell the home. Their savvy lawyer had seen that Rory would receive nothing if that happened. Didn't matter. However the media slanted it, Rory had never cared about the money or other material possessions.

Pete and teaching had been her world. Austin had already been away at university, and Lulu, well, Lulu was Lulu. The eccentric lady had been all over the place and always running off to visit friends in other locations for days or weeks. Rory hoped some of those friends had taken the time to visit her while she was ill with cancer. Given all that had happened, Rory hadn't even thought to ask her brother.

With the tour over, Chance parked in the driveway of Lulu's place. Rory exhaled a big breath as they emerged from the car. The plywood remained on the damaged window. She would get around to the repair eventually. There were more important issues to worry about just now.

Digging into her back pocket, she produced the house key. She really needed to rummage around in her things for a handbag. At some point she would go for a new driver's license. Or maybe not. Really there was no point, she supposed, until she knew how this new investigation was going to turn out. If she was forced to return to prison, she certainly wouldn't need a license to drive.

The mere thought of going back twisted inside her like barbed wire.

The key slid into the lock, and Rory gave it a turn. Inside was a little stuffy. They'd closed and locked the windows, revealing that Lulu's air-conditioning was struggling to do its job. By next month, the house would be an oven. She should call a repairman and see what the damage would be. Not that she had any money to speak of. But Lulu had left a small sum in her bank account. Rory had been added to the account years ago so technically she could use it. It seemed reasonable to use Lulu's money on her beloved little cottage—she'd called it a cottage. And it was, sort of, at least in size. As for style, Lulu had given it plenty.

Chance came in right behind her, carrying the bags from her favorite Chinese restaurant. The place had been in the same location just off the square for as long as she could remember. The husband-and-wife team who owned and operated the quaint little place had remembered her. She and Lulu had been regulars. The couple's kind response to seeing her gave Rory a glimmer of hope. Maybe there actually were a few people who didn't want her to go directly back to jail.

Rory supposed the couple could be added to the column of happy-to-see-her. That made about three if she included Austin.

Chance left the bags on the kitchen table. "I'll get my laptop, and we can go over interviews and the autopsy report if you're up to it."

She nodded, slowly. "Sure." The idea of the autopsy

report made her hesitate. Made her feel uneasy. But it was just another part of this painful journey.

It was important to use every opportunity to discuss the case. How else would they find anything? For all she knew, Detective Fowler could show up at her door any time to say that he was arresting her again. But Jamie Colby had assured Rory that would not happen until the investigation was fully prepared to proceed. The DA's office would not want to go back to trial without all their ducks in a row, so to speak.

While Chance readied his laptop, she removed the containers of entrées from the bags. She grabbed a couple of plates and then bottles of water from the fridge. Since Chance was still working with his laptop, she went ahead and divvied up portions of noodles, egg rolls, sweet and sour chicken and Szechwan pork. It smelled amazing.

"Thank you." He turned to the plate she'd placed in front of him.

She held up chopsticks and a plastic fork. "Do you have a preference?"

"Either one works for me."

She passed him the chopsticks and reached back into the bag for her own. As quickly as she could navigate those chopsticks, Rory stuffed a wad of noodles into her mouth and closed her eyes, savoring the flavors.

When she opened her eyes, he was grinning at her. "That must be really good."

She put her hand in front of her mouth to prevent him watching her chew while she said, "So, so good."

He lifted his chopsticks to his lips and slurped noodles into his mouth. "Mmm. You're right."

Reminding herself not to stare, she poked in another

bite. The spicy goodness made her cheeks flush. It was just the heat of the food. Not Chance. Not at all.

He'd said they would talk about the case while they ate, but either they were too hungry to slow down, or the food was just too good to detract from it with conversation. Didn't take long, though, for Rory to feel stuffed. Prison meals were not so good, and portions weren't exactly generous.

She leaned back in her chair and sighed. "That was awesome."

Chance finished off a bite and did the same. "No wonder that's your favorite restaurant."

"Pete and I picked up take-out from there at least once a week, sometimes twice. I tried but could never prepare any of the dishes on the menu even close to the way they do."

"You like to cook?" he asked.

"Sometimes." She shrugged. "Lulu and I liked trying to replicate our favorite restaurant dishes." The thought made her smile. "It was an adventure every time."

"I can see how that would be a challenge." Chance stood, disposed of his remains and put the plate in the sink.

Rory recognized that was her cue to get down to business. She took her plate to the sink. No need for a stop at the trash bin—she'd practically licked the plate clean.

When she resumed her seat once more at the table, Chance was already reviewing something on his laptop.

"The owner of the White Cottage was interviewed, as were your closest neighbors, coworkers, friends and family." His gaze settled on hers. "A lot of people were questioned."

She remembered well those endless discussions of what

was said and who said it. "None could point to anything that suggested Pete and I had problems of any kind. No one had ever witnessed an argument between us. Neither he nor I ever complained to friends or coworkers about the other or our relationship."

Chance studied her a moment. "The two of you never fought. Never disagreed. Even in private."

"We disagreed occasionally, yes." She gave a single, firm nod. "But we never argued or fought. We talked it out, and if either of us grew too emotional, we set the subject aside. When we felt ready, we revisited it."

His eyebrows lifted slightly. "That sounds very...polite."

Her lips trembled just a little before she could stop the outward display. "Pete was like that. Always polite. Always thoughtful of others' feelings."

Still obviously unconvinced, he braced his forearms on the table. "I'm wondering how a man in his position at such a large development company could be so sensitive...so *not* pushy. Scheduling issues, personnel problems, contract negotiations. How'd he handle the ups and downs of the business?"

"The answer to that one is easy." She pressed her lips together a moment, thinking back on Pete's thoughts on the matter. "Pete always said his parents were the pushy ones. He didn't want a marriage like theirs. As for the business, if there were problems at work, Pete handled them calmly and professionally. Surprisingly it worked better, in his opinion. I think people were so grateful not to have to deal with Anthony that they worked out any issues with Pete rather than the alternative."

She'd often wondered how two people so ambitious and, frankly, pushy ever had a son like Pete.

Chance's attention lingered on the laptop screen again. "It would seem his actions backed up his words. Every person interviewed by the police said he was the nicest guy they'd ever met."

It was more difficult to keep the tremble from her lips this time. "That was Pete."

Chance stared at the table a moment before meeting her gaze once more. "I don't want you to take this the wrong way," he began, "but everyone has a darker side, maybe not very dark, but a little unpleasant at the very least. Everyone has bad thoughts occasionally. Everyone makes mistakes. What I'm finding in the statements and hearing from you is that Pete seemed perfect, and we both know that's not possible."

Rory wanted to shout at him. To shake him. Something to make him see that he simply didn't understand. Pete was this amazing and, yes, perfect guy. He was so nice. So sweet. She couldn't explain it. He just was.

When she'd tamped down the initial reaction, she said, "I understand what you're saying. But it's true. Pete and I started dating, and two months later we moved in together. Four months after that, we got married. *Six months.* I knew him for six months. I lived with him for four of those months. Don't you think if he had any sort of dark side, I would have seen at least a glimpse of it?"

"Maybe." He smiled, the expression sad. "Understand that I have to ask these questions. There is a reason this happened. A motive. If Pete hadn't crossed anyone and you hadn't crossed anyone, that leaves only two options— a random act of violence for nothing other than the thrill of the kill, or the one Detective Fowler believes."

That Rory killed her husband.

Emotions swelled and knotted inside her. "Well, we can cross out that last one, because I did not kill my husband."

He nodded. "Okay. Let's move on. The next anomaly we need to consider is why you were left alive."

She clasped her fingers together to prevent picking at her cuticles or some other nervous fidgeting. "I've asked myself that a million times. I was in and out of consciousness, so I can only assume something happened to make them leave before they could kill me. I wasn't bleeding anywhere. I had no broken bones. Just bruises and scratches and a concussion. Obviously I was in no danger of dying. They had to understand that was the case."

That part—her being left alive—remained a total mystery to her. She often wondered if it would have been easier if she'd died too.

Don't even go there.

Chance rubbed a hand over his jaw, cupped his chin for a moment. "Are you certain Pete had nothing from work with him? Nothing of value that you may not have known about, like a jump drive or file or key to a safety deposit box? Something the intruders came for but didn't want it to be obvious. That's what the break-in was about. It's possible the intrusion wasn't about the two of you at all, but something related to the business or the Harris family."

A frown tugged at her. "I suppose that's possible, but why wouldn't Anthony bring it up during the investigation? He loved his son. I can't imagine that he wouldn't do everything possible to uncover who killed him."

"Except," Chance countered, "Anthony and Eudora thought they had their killer."

Her shoulders sagged. "True." Not only had she been falsely accused, but she was likely the reason they hadn't looked further for the real killer.

"I want you," Chance urged, "to think about that scenario. Try and recall if Pete mentioned anything about an issue with a business contract or negotiation or a person related to work. Or some big coup or change coming."

"Okay. I will say, though," she offered, "that he rarely talked about work unless it was something he wanted to celebrate with me. Whatever problems the business had, he left at work. He said his father had been bad to bring work issues home, and Pete never wanted to do that to me."

Chance chuckled. "You're right. I'm beginning to think the guy was perfect."

Rory inhaled a big breath. This next part wouldn't be so easy. Not that any of it was, really. But some parts were admittedly harder than others. Like going back to White Cottage.

"You said you had a copy of the autopsy report." She held her breath in an effort to slow the frantic beating of her heart. This was a part she never liked thinking about.

"Yeah." He nodded. "But I don't think you want to look at it. There's just one image that I would like you to see, and I can arrange for that one to lessen the impact."

"Okay." She wouldn't argue. She had no desire to see the accompanying photos or to read the cold, somber descriptions of her husband's injuries.

He tapped a few keys and then turned the screen around for her to see. She blinked, studied the image closer. This was her husband's neck, the left side, she decided. True to his word, Chance had resized the image so that nothing except a patch of skin was visible. Her heart ached just knowing that this was part of him…that the rest of the image likely showed his dead body.

"You see these marks?" Chance tapped the screen.

She steadied herself and looked more closely. There were two small circular marks. Reddish in color. There was some amount of bruising on the skin around them. "What are those?"

"Taser marks," Chance explained. "See the bruising?" He tapped the screen again. "You only get that when whoever is holding the Taser presses it really hard into the skin."

Rory flinched. "But there was nothing mentioned about a Taser. I didn't own a Taser, and neither did Pete."

"Even stranger," Chance pointed out as he closed the laptop, "there is no mention of those marks anywhere in the ME's report."

Rory swallowed, her throat suddenly dry. "But that shouldn't have been left out, right? I mean, it's relevant to the overall condition of the…*body*, if not to the cause of death."

"That is exactly right."

"When…" She moistened her lips. "When the photo isn't blown up the way you showed it to me, are the marks still easy to see? Maybe he missed them. I'm pretty sure the medical examiner is an older man."

Chance smiled patiently. "The ME's job is to find the smallest anomaly. He wouldn't have missed anything. I imagine he has an assistant who helped. In my opinion, he either left it out on purpose, or whoever typed the final report accidentally left it out when transcribing his dictation."

"There was no mention of it in the courtroom." She would have remembered any mention of unusual marks on her husband's body. Rory rubbed at her forehead with her fingers. She was so tired, and another headache was threatening. "I know we have to talk about all these things." She lifted her gaze to his. "But it feels like we're getting nowhere. I mean, we know there were holes in the investigation, and now we find a discrepancy in the medical examiner's report, but what do we do with any of this? Point it out to Detective Fowler? Go to the media?"

"We go to the source. We go to the ME about his report. We go to Detective Fowler, and we ask him about the discrepancies in his work."

The idea of going to Fowler made her stomach churn. But she would have Chance at her side. "Okay." She squared her shoulders. "What if they both refuse to discuss the case with us?"

"Then we go around them. Trust me, Rory, I have never met a roadblock I couldn't get around."

Hearing him say those words was an immense relief.

"There's something else," he said.

Rory braced for more bad news. "What else?"

"I've been meaning to talk to you about my lodging arrangements."

She grimaced. "Is the motel that bad?" It wasn't exactly a five-star accommodation.

"No, it's fine. My concern is leaving you here alone. I would feel more comfortable staying here with you." He held up his hands stop-sign fashion as if he expected her to launch a counterattack. "I understand that isn't the most comfortable scenario, but after what happened last night, I just don't think you being here alone is a good idea."

She blew out a breath, relief washing through her. "I would love for you to stay. Please stay."

He smiled, gave her a nod. "Good. I believe this is the best way to ensure your safety. Would you mind riding to the motel with me to pick up my bag?"

"Sure." She stood. "There's a Dairy Dip just down the street from the motel. I could use a milkshake."

He grinned as he pushed to his feet. "Let me guess. Strawberry?"

"No way." She laughed. "Chocolate. Always."

He laughed, and they walked out of the house together. When she'd locked up, they loaded into his car. She studied his profile while he drove. For the first time in over two years, she felt a little lighter, a little...*almost* happy. And she had this man to thank for it. She wondered if all Colby Agency investigators were as nice as Chance. He was very nice and very handsome. She liked him.

A frown tugged at her lips. She turned away, stared out the window.

When Pete died, she had been certain she would never look at another man and feel anything. Were these unexpected glimmers of happiness and hope just a part of the adrenaline related to trying to find the truth? Maybe she was suffering from some kind of protector syndrome.

Whatever the case, she turned back to Chance, glad he was here.

Chapter Ten

Wednesday, June 17

Patterson Law Office
Laurel Street
Scottsboro, 9:00 a.m.

The decision was made last night that they would start with her attorney. Rory was glad. He'd been oddly silent since her return. No visit, not even a phone call. It was time to confront him and demand an explanation.

Rory was thankful for a good night's sleep. Something about knowing Chance was in the next room had put her completely at ease. She had known she was safe. This morning breakfast had been relaxed, not strained or uncomfortable. Really, she continued to be surprised by how easy he was to be around.

Shaking off the thoughts, Rory took a deep breath and readied herself for today's agenda to begin. Maybe this would be the day they found something that helped her case. What better place to start than with the attorney who had defended her?

Gerald "Gerry" Patterson had been the only attorney in the area who would take Rory's case. Since at the time she still had a job and some assets related to her marriage, she hadn't qualified for a court-appointed attorney. But Mr. Patterson had, somewhat reluctantly, stepped up to the plate. Rory had surmised based on the tension sparking between her Aunt Lulu and Patterson that there was leverage of some sort. Leverage she wielded mercilessly. Lulu never said, much less explained, but Rory suspected the two had been involved at some point over the years.

Evidently Patterson had not wanted his wife to learn about whatever his and Lulu's involvement amounted to. Whatever the case, the past had not been Rory's concern at that moment. Her husband had been murdered, and no one had believed the truth she was telling them.

How did she make anyone believe her if there was no evidence? She had desperately needed someone capable of gathering their own evidence. Of finding what no one else did. But Patterson had turned out not to be that man. He had been and was still only a small-town attorney with little ambition, a secretary and a clerk currently enrolled in law school. Nothing wrong with small. She wondered sometimes if his lackluster performance had been more about nearing retirement or resentment that he'd been forced to take a case that would not gain him anything but trouble.

What she had needed—Rory glanced at the man who had just parked in front of the attorney's office—had been someone like Chance Rader and the Colby Agency. But she hadn't known at the time that the truth wouldn't set her free. Foolishly, she had believed the facts would be uncovered and the bad guys would be caught and punished. Who in the world could possibly have believed for a moment that she would murder her husband?

Apparently a lot of people.

She had greatly underestimated the power of the Harris name. Not for her—a Harris by marriage only—but for her in-laws. Worse, in Rory's opinion, why had Eudora and Anthony not wanted to find the truth? How could they possibly have been so convinced she was guilty?

Grief, she supposed. That level of grief did things to people. Obliterated common sense. Destroyed all reason and logic. And maybe the pain had been so all consuming that having it over was more important than the truth.

"You ready?"

Rory blinked and met his gaze. "Yes. I was just thinking." She shook her head. "Sometimes I just can't fully grasp how this happened."

He smiled, the expression sad or resigned. "Bad things happen to good people. Sadly, more often than you think. But we are going to turn this around." He tapped his temple. "The wheels are turning, and scenarios are forming."

She dredged up a smile of her own. "Maybe I'll get lucky, and we'll go in this office and find out that my attorney—the one who took my meager life's savings—will have come up with a few scenarios as well."

Chance chuckled. "We can always hope."

Rory got out of the car and met him at the sidewalk. The one thing the Colby Agency and Chance had given her already in the short period of their involvement was hope. Two years ago, she had lost all hope. She had felt so lost and forlorn, she hadn't really cared what happened to her.

But she had new hope now. She was not going back to that prison, and she was not giving up on herself again.

The law office opened at nine. Chance opened the door for Rory at 9:02. They hadn't made an appointment. Chance felt it was best not to give Patterson too much time to line up his excuses. Better to catch him off guard. Rory was only too happy to go along with the suggestion. She wouldn't mind seeing a little uncomfortable squirming after how the man had failed her.

Reba Johnson looked up and smiled for Chance. "Good morning." Then her gaze settled on Rory, and the smile faded. "Rory. You're home. Gerry has been expecting to hear from you."

Rory worked up a facsimile of a smile. "It's good to be home. I've been expecting to hear from him as well."

She should be nicer. After all, it was this office that found the issue that allowed her conviction to be overturned. Although it wasn't her attorney who'd discovered the withheld evidence, it was his clerk. The law school student, Leonard Wade.

Rory glanced at the empty desk a few feet away from Reba's. Apparently the secretary noticed. "Leonard is on vacation." Her smile widened to something visibly fake. "He'd always wanted to go to Cancun. He and his girlfriend won't be back for two weeks."

Rory told herself his absence had nothing to do with the timing of her release. But she couldn't help feeling that way. She remembered well the day Leonard visited her. He'd never done that before. The man, who was a year younger than Rory, had been vibrating with excitement. He'd found something, and with his boss, Patterson, out of town, he couldn't wait for Rory to hear the news. He was certain the discovery was just the first step toward clearing her name.

Sometimes she wondered if she would have ever been told about the evidence the DA's office had suppressed if Patterson had been in town. She disliked feeling that way, but she had suspected it was true. If Patterson could have gotten in front of it, no one would have ever known.

But now the game had changed. Now the race for the detective and the newly assigned DA was to find out where the fibers had come from as well as to find any additional evidence that Rory actually killed her husband. She wasn't sure how they would do either, but she certainly didn't intend to wait around and see.

"Did you need to see Gerry?" Reba asked, drawing Rory back to the moment.

"Yes." She wondered why the woman thought she was here if not to see Patterson. "I'm sure we have things to discuss."

"Of course," Reba agreed with that too-wide smile on her lips. She gestured to the chairs that lined the wall on the other side of the small lobby. "Just have a seat, and I'll let him know you're here."

Rory lowered into one of the chairs, Chance chose the one next to her. He turned his face to hers and spoke for her ears only. "Frankly, I'm surprised he wasn't at the prison when you were released."

The fact was that beyond the notification she was being released, she hadn't heard from Gerry. "I suppose the situation complicates things for him."

Her gaze settled on the clerk's desk once more. This still felt like a strange time for Leonard to be away. Rory had been released because of his find. Why wouldn't he want to be here reveling in his big win? Maybe Patterson had fired him.

Reba breezed back into the room. "Go on in, y'all." That broad smile rested on Rory once more. "He's excited to see you, Rory."

She fixed her lips into an answering smile and thanked the woman.

Gerry Patterson stood behind his desk, wearing his own big smile. He lifted his arms in welcome like a reverend would for his congregation. "Come in, come in," he said. "Rory, this must be Mr. Chance Rader from the Colby Agency."

Chance reached across the desk and offered his hand. "Good to meet you, sir."

Patterson shook his hand firmly, then gestured for them to sit. "Your brother," he said to Rory, "explained that the Colby Agency would be assisting us this go around." He sent a nod in Chance's direction as he resumed his seat behind the cluttered desk. "We're sure glad to have you. This is a delicate situation for all concerned."

"Well," Chance said, "my agency and I hope to help change that. We've already determined a number of holes in the investigation. Frankly, I'm surprised the case got to trial so quickly considering the minimal evidence against your client."

"Well, her prints were on the knife," Patterson reminded him. "There was no evidence found to suggest anyone else was ever in the cottage."

Fury spread through Rory so fast she barely remained seated. She clenched her jaw to prevent shouting at the man. Chance would handle this with far more diplomacy than she could possibly summon given the attorney's attitude.

"What about the basket of food?" Chance queried. "There were no prints other than Rory's and her husband's found on it?"

"Basket?" He frowned as if he wasn't sure what Chance meant.

"There was a basket," Rory explained, barely stifling her outrage, "packed the way you would a picnic basket with the bread, cheeses and champagne."

Patterson frowned. "Oh, yes. I remember. Well, obviously there were no other prints found. The report said as much."

"Obviously," Chance said, drawing Patterson's attention to him, "the report was wrong." He held the man's gaze without speaking long enough for Patterson to finally realize what he was getting at.

"Are you suggesting there may have been prints that were overlooked?"

"There had to be," Rory said, frustration taking away her ability to restrain herself. "Austin brought the basket to the cottage for us before we arrived that night. His prints must have been on the door and were certainly on the basket—at the very least."

The attorney's entire face furrowed this time as he seemed to mull over her words. "Perhaps they ruled him out since he was your brother and had an alibi. He and your aunt had dinner together that evening, I believe."

"They did, yes," Chance agreed. "But the invasion into White Cottage didn't happen until hours later."

Tension rippled through Rory. What was he saying? She stared at his profile, waiting for him to explain.

"I'm not implying," Chance went on, "that Austin had anything to do with what happened. My point is that if they missed his prints or left them out of evidence, then that's another failure on their part. Due diligence requires that they consider all avenues, particularly ones for which they have evidence."

Patterson cleared his throat. "I see your point. Obviously, the detective failed to do all that he should have."

"It rained that night," Rory spoke up, needing to move on from even the most remote notion that her brother was involved. "The rain was never brought up. There may have been footprints around the house that were overlooked." Tire prints weren't likely since the street and the parking area were all paved.

Patterson nodded slowly. "I can look into that."

Outrage lashed through Rory. Why hadn't he looked into it before? She wished she had been able to talk to Leonard today. He might have known about that too, but anything else he might have discovered never made it to Rory or into the appeal.

"There's one other thing," Chance said then. "The autopsy report makes no mention of Taser marks on the victim's body."

Patterson eyebrows reared up. "What Taser mark? There was never any mention of a Taser at trial." He looked to Rory. "Have you remembered something you didn't mention before?"

She shook her head. "No. Mr. Rader found the discrepancy in the autopsy report. Apparently no one else noticed."

Her words hit the mark. Red climbed up the attorney's throat and spread across his face. His jaw worked for a moment before he was able to speak. "I'll need to review the report to refresh my memory."

Rory wanted to demand why he hadn't already refreshed his memory.

"You'll see the mark in the photos." Chance gestured to his neck. "About here on the right side. Whoever used the Taser was likely right-handed."

Patterson grabbed a pen and made a note of what he'd just been told.

"What sort of follow up are you doing on the undisclosed fibers?" Chance inquired.

The attorney seemed to draw himself up slightly straighter. "I've asked for the full forensic report."

"You haven't received it yet?" The surprise in Chance's voice was clear. "Have you requested a sample to send to an outside lab?"

Patterson held up a hand. "One moment." He picked up the phone on his desk and punched a button. "Reba, can you step into my office for a moment?" He cleared his throat again. "We'll get the ball rolling on that."

Rory exchanged a look with Chance. This was either incompetence or indifference. She wasn't sure which one was worse, but she couldn't afford either.

Reba hustled into the office. She glanced around at the parties seated. "Yes, sir?"

Patterson peered up at her with a questioning look that was obviously exaggerated. "Have we received the forensic report on those fibers related to Rory's case?"

It was the blink…the blank expression and the three-second delay in her response that gave Rory the answer. They hadn't asked for the report. Or, at the very least, had not followed up on the request.

"We have not, no. But I'll get in touch with the DA's office right now and find out what the holdup is," she assured her boss, then hurried back to her desk, closing the door behind her.

"Do you plan," Chance said, drawing the attorney's attention back to him, "to re-interview any of the character witnesses?"

"Oh, yes." He nodded adamantly. "We're lining those up already. I'll be sure to pass along whatever we find."

Rory couldn't take the lies and the excuses anymore.

She stood. "Well, thank you, Mr. Patterson. I look forward to hearing from you sooner rather than later."

She marched out of his office, her fury barely in check. Chance followed. As difficult as it was, she somehow managed to hold back the words she wanted to shout until they were in the car.

"Does he really believe," she exclaimed, her back against the seat, her attention focused on the office front window only a dozen or so feet away, "that I won't notice his disregard for my situation? His total lack of interest in how this goes?"

Chance reached for the hand she had braced on the console. He gave it a squeeze. "What you need is a new attorney."

She closed her eyes. How on earth was she supposed to make that happen? She had no money for a new attorney, and the process for being assigned a court-ordered one would eat up valuable time. Time they might not have. "I can't..." She blinked back the burn of damned tears.

"If you're in agreement, the agency will have someone take over the case," he assured her. "You and I are not going to worry about anything except finding the evidence we need to make sure this never goes back to trial."

Rory almost wept with relief. "That would mean the world to me."

He nodded. "Done."

She drew in a deep breath, let it go. "So what do we do now?" She turned to him and held on tightly to his hand.

"Now we go see someone who worked with Pete. Whoever you believe may have known about any work-related issues. We need to rule that scenario out so we can focus on the next one."

Rory nodded. "I know just the guy to talk to." She

waited until he'd backed from the parking slot. "What's the next one? I mean, after we talk to Pete's work friend?"

He met her gaze, held it for three beats. "The possibility that someone close to Pete wanted him out of the way."

Chapter Eleven

The Docks
Hembree Drive
Scottsboro, 12:00 p.m.

The restaurant wasn't particularly swanky, but it was on the water, and the food was good. The atmosphere was casual with lots of wood and metal decor that spoke of relaxing and spending time on the water, whether fishing or just boating. Or, in this case, dining.

"Can I help you, folks?" the cashier behind the counter asked. "You're welcome to sit wherever you please."

"Thank you. We're here to meet a friend." Not exactly a lie, Rory told herself.

Louis Larson sat at the booth that Pete had once told her was the company's booth. The owner of The Docks had actually placed a small brass plaque on the window trim above the table dubbing it the "Harris Corp" table. Of course, the table was open to anyone, but whenever someone from the company was here, this was where they were seated. Maybe in part because they had generously donated to the owner's startup back in the day.

Pete had loved this place. He and a couple of his closest colleagues dropped in for lunch regularly.

"That's him." Rory nodded to the blond man seated alone in the farthest corner of the dining room in that designated booth. "Louis is thirty-five. He's been with the company since he graduated with his master's in finance. Pete always said he was the best financial whiz on the team—maybe in the state."

"Let's join him." Chance looked to her to make the next move.

Rory led the way to the booth and paused. "Hello, Louis."

He looked up from his meal. Surprise flared in his eyes. "Rory." He scrambled to get out of the booth and stood for a moment just staring at her. "You are here." He made a sound of wonder as if he still couldn't believe his eyes. "I read that you were back, but I…" He shook his head and then awkwardly hugged her.

Rory was so startled that he would even touch her that she wasn't sure what to do with her hands.

When he drew back, Rory said, "It's good to see you." Louis glanced at the man standing next to her. "This is Chance Rader," she explained. "He's working with my new attorney to sort out this mess."

Chance extended his hand. "Good to meet you, Mr. Larson."

The two shook hands, Louis still appearing a little befuddled.

"Please." He gestured to the booth. "Join me."

Rory slipped into the bench seat, making room for Chance to sit next to her. Louis slid into his seat and stared at her for another moment. Then he exhaled a big breath and shook his head yet again. "This is…a very nice surprise."

His words were code for a shockingly awkward situation in which he didn't know what to do or say. The part of him that had liked Pete wanted to be kind, but that same part wanted to lash out at her. All those emotions were easy to read on his face.

"I apologize for showing up uninvited like this," she offered. "I'm sure this must be awkward for you, but I need your help."

He held up his hands. "Rory, let me stop you right there." He searched her face before he spoke. "I don't know what happened that night. But I do know that Pete loved you with everything he had. You were his world. And I know that he wouldn't want me to be unkind to you. Ever."

Tears sprang on her lashes so quickly she barely held them back. "I loved him exactly the same way. I would never in a million years have hurt him."

Louis nodded as if he understood. "Tell me how I can help."

A waitress appeared. "Can I get you folks anything?"

"Maybe later," Chance said, and she drifted away.

Rory reset her attention on Louis. "Was there anything going on with work—a client maybe—who might have had an issue with Pete?" She shrugged. "It's a stretch, I realize, but I'm desperate to find anything that might explain how this happened. I want to find the people responsible for his death."

He nodded slowly, considering her question. "Detective Fowler came to me maybe a week after it happened. He asked me to think long and hard on that same question. But I'll tell you exactly what I told him. The company was running as smooth as glass. There were no issues. No schedules or contracts were behind. No trouble with clients. Nothing. Believe me when I say, if there had been anything at all that suggested even a hint of concern, I would have been the first one to speak up."

Rory couldn't help feeling deflated. She had felt confident there were no issues with work, but she'd dared to hope. And, honestly, the fact that Fowler had bothered to look into the possibility surprised her. "Thank you, Louis. I really appreciate you confirming what I already believed."

"If I may," Chance said, "what about Mr. Harris, Pete's father?"

"Oh." Louis made a face of confusion. "He was devastated, of course. In my opinion, he still hasn't gotten over losing his son."

"I'm certain he hasn't," Chance agreed. "My query is related to where he stood on the marriage. There were some issues in the family when Pete decided to marry Rory. Did any of that come up around that same time? Were Pete and his father on good terms given the circumstances?"

Rory saw the shift in Louis's eyes immediately. He had been a dear friend to Pete, but he was also loyal to the Harris family as well as the company. He would not want to speak unkindly about Anthony or Eudora.

"They had a difficult time for a while when Pete announced his intentions." Louis directed a smile at Rory. "But I think that was more about fear than anything else. Pete was a good son. Eudora and Anthony only wanted the best for him. Sometimes even great parents make mistakes." He shifted his attention to Chance. "To answer your question, I did not note any unusual tension—or tension at all for that matter—between Pete and his parents."

"Thank you, Mr. Larson." Chance turned to Rory for the next move.

"We should let you finish your lunch," she offered.

"Please," he argued, "join me. My treat."

It was lunchtime. Rory looked to Chance, who gave her a nod of agreement. "Thank you," she said to Louis. "That would be very nice."

Just maybe, they would learn something else.

Except she feared there was nothing to learn. Pete had no enemies. It was quite possibly time she admitted that his murder was not about him or his family. It was about her.

Jackson County Park
County Park Road
Scottsboro, 2:00 p.m.

CHANCE STOOD WITH her on the dock where she and Pete had held their ceremony.

His parents had been disappointed. They had wanted the ceremony in their backyard and, granted, it would have been beautiful, but Rory and Pete had known that if Eudora had control of the wedding on her home turf, it would have turned into something huge and complicated. They hadn't wanted a big wedding or anything complicated. No fanfare. Just the opportunity to share the first step into their future with those closest to them.

The dress had been the most complex part of the wedding. It had been the perfect fairy-tale dress. The one she had always wanted. Handmade by her dear Aunt Lulu. Honestly, it had been too much for their small lakeside ceremony, but it had felt perfect. Rory would never forget that day.

It wasn't until after dark that it turned into a nightmare.

"It's peaceful here," Chance said.

She nodded. "It is. My aunt used to bring my brother and me here all the time as kids. It was free, and there were all sorts of interesting places to explore." She laughed. "Free always fit the budget."

For a long while, they said nothing, just stared out over the calm water. Several emotions whirled inside Rory, but she didn't want to think about any of that right now. She needed to clear her head. To put some distance between her and what she felt sure was the truth she so desperately wanted to deny.

"Did Eudora and Anthony seem at all happy during the ceremony?" Chance turned to her. "Or was the animosity obvious?"

"I'd just found out that week about the offer she'd made to try and dissuade Pete from marrying me. I could barely look at her." She rolled her eyes. "What kind of mother does that?"

"You would be surprised." Chance tucked his hands into his pockets. "From what you've told me, Pete was an easy-going guy. His mother had probably been in charge for most of his life—even his adult life, since he worked in the family business. Lived in the same town."

"You know, I never considered how that must have stifled him. I can't even imagine living under someone's thumb like that." Rory laughed. The abrupt sound just burst out of her when she considered the irony in what she'd related without thinking. "What am I saying? I just spent nearly two years in prison. I am very well aware of what it feels like to be stifled."

Chance smiled. He had the nicest smile. Rory banished the thought that popped into her head every single time the man's lips turned up. She had to stop looking at him that way. This was a business relationship. Her future depended on how this turned out. As desperately as she needed a hero like him, he wasn't here to comfort her… only to help her find the truth and to support her efforts to prove her innocence.

"Any inkling that Anthony felt the same way as his wife?" Chance closed his eyes and turned his face up to the sun.

Rory started to do the same, but she got caught up in watching him relish the sunlight. "I never noticed anything." She thought about the man that was her father-in-law for only a few hours. "He kept quiet as far as I know. I'm sure he was on her side. I mean, she was his wife. My impression was that Anthony wanted his wife to be happy. He didn't do things to hinder that end."

Chance looked at her then. "Makes his life more bearable, wouldn't you think?"

"I suppose so." She closed her eyes and lifted her face to the sun this time. The warmth felt so good. A week ago she would have given most anything to be standing close to the water enjoying the sun's brilliance like this.

But how long would it last?

"What about your boyfriends before Pete?" he asked, drawing her attention back to him. "Any serious relationships? Maybe someone who didn't want to let go?"

"Let's sit," she suggested, suddenly too weary to keep standing. Or maybe she just needed not to have this conversation in the sunlight, which suddenly felt too harsh.

Chance followed her back to the shore and to a grouping of shade trees where benches and picnic tables waited. Rory perched on one and set her gaze back on the water. Whispers from the past, her and Austin running around and laughing, sifted through her mind. Even after losing their parents, they had somehow managed to find happiness. There was that one time when they were playing and Lulu had been chatting with a friend. Austin had fallen off that very dock where Rory's wedding ceremony took place. Without thought, she had jumped into the water and dragged her little brother to safety.

Rory shuddered at the memory. Now her little brother was attempting to rescue her. With effort, she pushed away the past and focused on the question Chance had asked.

"There were a few boyfriends over the years. I never allowed myself to get too deeply involved. I realized how important it was that I get my education and start a career." She laughed softly. "There's nothing like being poor to keep you motivated."

"No dramatic relationships during the high school or college years?"

"None at all. Lulu kept telling me I was pushing myself too hard. I was too serious. I needed to have fun. Get into a little trouble." Rory smiled. "I never got into trouble. Never cheated on a test. Never stole so much as a piece of gum. Lulu always looked at me as if she worried I wasn't even related to her."

"You were a nice girl."

"Losing our parents the way we did, I think it changes you."

He watched her closely as she spoke. She should have been nervous, but somehow she wasn't. Talking to Chance felt easy…good. She needed good and certainly would take a little easy after the past couple of years.

"Some people change in a bad way," she went on. "They become depressed or maybe indifferent after a tragedy. They lash out. Stop caring about anything. Others go the route Austin and I did. We hunkered down and worked diligently to make the best out of an unhappy situation. I think we were too hurt, too scared to do anything else."

It wasn't until she said the words that she realized how they sounded. "Not because Lulu was mean to us or didn't take care of us," she explained, "but just because it felt like the world had changed, and we had to be careful or something else bad would happen." She turned to Chance. "I remember praying so hard. Promising to be extra good if God would just please, please take care of my brother. I was terrified of losing him. He had the same fears about me. It was so sad for a very long time."

"Eventually," Chance nudged, "you got stronger and had a serious relationship."

Good grief. She'd gotten completely off track. "Yes, but just one. About a year before I met Pete, there was a very nice fellow teacher from the high school, Kevin Warren. We dated for nearly a year." She thought of the night he'd proposed. "I felt so bad when it ended abruptly, but I'd met Pete and it was, I swear, love at first sight. I mean really, very intense. There was no going back."

"You broke off the relationship with Kevin and started dating Pete."

"I did. It was the only time I felt like I really let someone down. He called for a while. Came by the house a few times, but he was never angry or unreasonable. He was hurt. But when he realized I wasn't changing my mind, he stopped. I was sad about how it ended for a while. I understood I had hurt him. Thankfully, later, we were able to see each other at school functions and not walk the other way. We didn't become friends, but we weren't enemies either. He got married, and the last I heard, there was a baby on the way. He got his happily-ever-after."

"I guess we can rule out Kevin," Chance commented.

"I think so." She smiled. "Really, my life was quite boring until that night." Her face scrunched with other bad memories. "Well, other than the fire."

"What do you remember about the fire?"

She was certain that fire and the death of her parents had nothing to do with Pete's murder, but for some reason she didn't mind sharing that part of her history with Chance. He'd probably read all the headlines and internet stories about it anyway.

"Saturday nights were movie night. We'd have popcorn and watch a movie, all while lying on the living room floor on blankets and quilts like we were camping." She drew in a deep breath. "It was cold, so my father had started a fire in the fireplace. I remember hours later my mother waking me up and guiding me to my room. Austin slept in the same room with me; Dad had carried him to his bed. It was really like any other Saturday night."

Chance watched her so closely, as if he were hanging on every word.

"I vaguely remember kisses on our cheeks. The wind blowing a limb against the window next to my bed. There was a big moon shining through the glass. I was so sleepy." She smiled. "My eyes kept closing. The next thing I knew, we were outside on the ground. It was so cold. I remember hearing my father scream my mother's name.

"Fire trucks were suddenly there…an ambulance. Police cars. There were all these lights flashing in the darkness. Mom and Dad were gone. Dead. It was just us, me and Austin. A policeman called Lulu. Things get a little foggy after that. I think I blocked as much as possible. Austin blocked even more because he was so young."

"I'm sorry, Rory," Chance said quietly. "I know that must have been really hard for you and Austin."

She nodded. "It was a nightmare that didn't end for years. Even when it did, we still missed our parents. But living with it got easier as the years passed." She turned to him. "You know, we were very close to where we lived back then when we visited Tay Banks. Another house was built in the spot. A long time ago."

"Thank you for sharing that with me."

They sat in silence for a while. Rory felt sure he was digesting all that she had told him. Eventually, he said, "I think our next step should be paying a visit to Leonard's house. Make sure he's really on vacation."

Rory hadn't considered that Patterson might lie about where he was, but it was obvious she couldn't trust the man. "You think Patterson lied to us?"

"It happens," he warned. "Some people—even lawyers—don't do well when backed into a corner."

"Okay, let's do it." She stood, then took a long look around the lake and the dock. Images from her wedding day flickered through her mind. It had been a beautiful day...at least until night came.

That night stole all the happiness from her life...took her heart and ripped it in two. Whoever had done this awful thing had gotten away with his evil deeds for far too long. She desperately wanted to find something that would point her in the right direction for uncovering the truth. For finding the real monster who destroyed her and Pete's lives.

She reminded herself that she and Chance had just begun and already were making progress. Patience was required no matter that it was difficult. But it was happening. Finally.

As they walked toward the car, a truck slowly rolled along the road that cut through the park. Rory reached her door, and Chance had already opened it. They both watched the truck roll closer. It looked vaguely familiar, had slowed considerably as if the driver intended to stop. Then it was right in front of them, and the driver threw up his hand in a wave.

Shane.

Rory frowned. Why would Shane Carter be driving by at this exact moment? She waved back at him, then got into the car. Maybe he was meeting someone at the barbecue place just on the other side of the park.

Chance started the engine and shifted into Drive. "Wasn't that Pete's cousin Shane?"

"It was." Maybe Shane felt compelled to keep an eye on her. He'd been helping out since she got home.

As they drove out of the park, she glanced over at the barbecue joint, but Shane's truck wasn't there. Maybe he'd met someone at one of the rental properties. The county park used to be the place for teenagers wanting to hang out and make out. Then again, Shane was no teenager anymore.

Maybe, she thought, Eudora and Anthony had enlisted his help in watching her. Eudora certainly liked being in control. Rory wouldn't put it past her to do exactly that. Shane had showed up at her place out of the blue. She wondered again how a wonderful man like Pete had such a wretched mother.

One of the world's great mysteries, she mused.

"You have an address for the clerk?"

"Yes, he lives on Franklin near where Pete and I lived before…"

"Headed that way," Chance said.

Rory mentally dissected the latest scenario that seemed the most likely explanation for what happened that awful night. She gave Chance the occasional direction for turns. But something about that scenario kept bugging her, snagging her attention.

"If what happened that night was somehow related to me," she said, turning to Chance, "why was Pete the one who died? Why not me?"

Chance looked to her for a moment before shifting his focus back to the street. "Sometimes, the best way to hurt a person is to take away what they love most."

His words blasted like tiny bombs in her brain. He was right. There was no more painful way to hurt a person. Dying a quick death—even a violent one—was over before you realized what was happening. You had little time for regrets or pain beyond the physical. But to be left alive while the person you loved most in the world was murdered…that was the worst possible pain, physical and emotional. Worse, it lingered, never truly went away.

Who would hate her so much that killing another human seemed a reasonable revenge for some perceived wrong?

The only person she suspected hated her that much was Eudora. No way in the world would she have killed her own son to punish Rory or to get her out of her life. She thought of all the times she had seen Pete and Eudora together. The woman was the epitome of the doting mother. She would have done anything for him…given him anything. There was no way in this world she would take his life.

Pete was *her* life.

Chapter Twelve

Wade Residence
Franklin Street
Scottsboro, 4:00 p.m.

Chance wasn't really surprised about Rory's attorney. The agency had found his work on the case to be lacking. Not falling to the level of inadequate from the law's perspective but less than it should have been—absolutely less than he was capable of providing. Had he done his best, the possibility that anything would have changed was largely unlikely. There simply had not been any evidence to support Rory's side of the story. While the other side had her prints on the murder weapon—a fact she could not explain. Her prints and the lack of story-confirming evidence had ensured the jury could only go one way— guilty. Patterson's failure had been in not doing more to sway that perception. Tangible evidence wasn't the only way to influence opinion.

Frankly, the man and his secretary had behaved a little on the suspicious side. Perhaps it was guilt. Whatever it was, the story about Leonard Wade, the clerk, suddenly going on vacation out of the country at the same time Rory was to be released didn't sit right with Chance. Leonard had been the one to find the single piece of evidence that could win the appeal. Why not be around for her release? Why not do interviews with the local media? What future attorney didn't want a little free publicity?

Didn't make a lot of sense for a guy trying to build experience for when he graduated law school and went out on his own.

"Doesn't look like anyone's home," Rory noted as she surveyed the yard and house.

There wasn't a garage. The midcentury brick rancher had a carport, but there was no vehicle parked there. Rory was correct. The place did look deserted. Maybe Patterson had been telling the truth.

"Only one way to find out." Chance reached for his door.

When they were standing on the driveway in front of his rental car, he took a moment to scan the block. Some of the houses along this section of the street had vehicles parked in the driveways. Farther down on the left, a lone dog barked, sending the occasional look in their direction. Otherwise, the street was quiet. No traffic, but then, it was well away from the main thoroughfares.

Rory led the way to the front door. She knocked and waited. The lack of sound inside added to the probability that no one was home.

Confident he wouldn't find anyone staring back at him, Chance went to the large window next to the door and had a look inside. The room he could see beyond lay in shadows since no lights were turned on. The only illumination came from the window where he stood. Despite the low visibility, it was obvious the space was empty. Not only of people but of anything. Furniture. Photos. Books. There was nothing in the room but the hardwood floor staring back at him.

Rory had knocked again. Chance turned to her. "I think we might have a bigger problem." He tilted his head toward the window. "Have a look."

She held his gaze, the dread and reluctance in her eyes shining through as she joined him at the window. With her hands cupped around her eyes, she leaned forward and peered inside. Almost immediately she drew back.

"His stuff is all gone." She shook her head. "I came by here once to leave a document for him. I've been in that room. There was a small sectional sofa. A television." Her head moved side to side again. "His grandmother left him this house." She scanned the yard again. "There's no For Sale sign. But maybe he moved. And… I…don't know. Why would Patterson lie about where he was?"

"The same reason he dropped the ball on your case, I suspect." Chance stepped away from the porch and had a look first on one side of the house, then the other. "We could ask a neighbor or go around back and look through a few more windows."

"Ask a neighbor," she suggested. "I'm not too keen on the idea of getting myself arrested if some attentive neighbor calls the police."

"Good point." He jerked his head to the right. "Let's try this one."

They walked back to the sidewalk rather than cross the yards and made their way to the next house. Rory had just knocked on the storm door when a vehicle passing on the street drew Chance's attention. It was the same truck from the park. Shane Carter's truck. This time the man didn't wave. He looked away quickly and sped up.

"The Carter guy just drove past again."

Rory followed his gaze and made a confused face.

"Why would he be following us and then just driving by? If he has something to tell me, why not stop or call me?"

"Good question."

Just then, the wood door behind the glass storm door opened. An elderly woman peered out at them. "If you're selling something," she grumbled, "you can just move along."

Rory smiled brightly no matter that she had little to smile about. "Hi, I'm a friend of Leonard's. I was hoping to catch him, but he doesn't seem to be home."

The woman frowned. "If you're a friend of his, why don't you know where he is?"

Chance bit back a grin. Savvy lady.

"I just got back in town," Rory explained. "I've been gone for a while, and I wanted to surprise him."

The woman's eyes narrowed, but then she appeared to relax. "Well, you won't find him around here. He moved."

"Really?" Rory shot Chance a look. "He's not just on vacation or something?" she asked the neighbor.

"Nope." She wagged her head side to side. "Last weekend he had a free-for-all going on over there. People was backing up in the grass and loading stuff up. He gave away all his furniture. When the people stopped coming, I went out there and asked him what was going on. He said he was moving, and he didn't want to take much of anything with him."

"Did he say where he was moving to?" Chance asked.

Her gaze narrowed again when she looked at Chance. "He did not. Just said he was moving on." She turned back to Rory. "A friend of mine at church who knows his mother said he was moving for work, but he didn't tell me that. Whatever his reason for moving, his mother was packing up to go with him. Seemed kind of odd to me.

One Sunday she was talking about the cantata she hoped to sing at church, and the next Sunday she's moving away."

"Thank you for telling me." Rory offered a smile that went nowhere near her eyes and turned away from the door.

Chance followed. When they were back in his car, he rested his attention on her. "We should talk to Patterson again, but first I'd like to visit with Carter and find out why he feels compelled to check in on us."

"I have his number," Rory said. "I added it to my contact list."

While she made the call, Chance considered that Carter might see him as some sort of threat to Rory. Or maybe the man was aware of some other potential threat but wasn't prepared to talk about it. There was also the possibility that he had a thing for Rory and didn't like another man getting in the way.

"He's not answering." Rory ended the call.

"Do you know where he lives?" Chance started the engine.

"Yes." She scoffed. "Well, I know where he lived two years ago."

As of now, Wade, Patterson and Shane Carter had claimed top spots on Chance's persons of interest list. The rub appeared to be in finding the reasons behind their actions.

There was always a reason. Always.

Carter Residence
Old Larkinsville Road
Scottsboro, 4:45 p.m.

THE MOBILE HOME where Shane Carter lived stood on a stretch of road flanked on one side by older homes, including Carter's, and on the other by railroad tracks. Since his truck wasn't in the driveway, it was safe to assume he wasn't home. But they were here. Might as well check it out.

When they parked in his driveway, Chance sent a text to his colleague, Max Granger, at the agency to run a deeper dive on Shane Carter and Leonard Wade. They'd already done so on Patterson. He was just a low-rent attorney with a fairly good case record. But he was barreling toward retirement age. Maybe his nest egg was lacking, and he'd decided his future was more important than Rory's.

The steps up to the small, uncovered porch at Carter's front door were a little rickety. Chance knocked on the door and listened for any sound coming from inside. Like Wade's house, there was nothing but silence.

"We're having no luck at all," Rory mentioned, clearly frustrated. "Kind of like me during the trial." She exhaled a big breath. "I had hoped that would change this time."

Chance sent her a smile. "It has. You just haven't seen the results yet."

She managed a smile back at him. "You're right. I need to be patient and not sound unappreciative of what you and the agency are doing."

"I get it," he assured her. "It's difficult to have patience when the stakes are so high."

Her cell phone rang. She jumped. "Good grief, I think that's the first time my phone has rung since Austin gave it to me."

She'd gotten text messages from her brother, but this was the first call Chance had heard. He hoped this wasn't the kind of call that would have her doubting his assurance that her luck was changing.

Her face paled as she listened to the caller.

So much for the value of his pep talk.

When the call ended, she met his gaze, hers worried. "That was Detective Fowler. He'd like me to come in for an interview. Right now."

"Don't worry. I'll be right there with you. This won't go the way it did two years ago."

His promise seemed to bolster her courage some as they returned to his car and headed back into town.

He wasn't actually surprised by the call. Quite possibly it was a good thing. It was time he and Rory got some feel for where the other side was going with the investigation this second go-around.

Not that he had any doubts about their intentions. They wanted Rory right back in that prison whether she was guilty or not.

But Chance and the Colby Agency were standing squarely in the way.

Chapter Thirteen

Scottsboro Police Department
South Broad Street
Scottsboro, 5:30 p.m.

Chance had said all the right things to shore up her confidence to the degree possible on the drive over. Still, Rory was so nervous. They waited in the lobby atrium. Seated together. Chance looking all calm and composed and Rory's foot tapping nervously, her hands knotted in her lap.

She felt like a ticking bomb ready to explode at any moment.

What if Detective Fowler was about to tell her they'd found some previously overlooked evidence that confirmed she was the murderer?

Rory closed her eyes. That was not possible because she was not a murderer. She had not hurt her husband, much less killed him. The only overlooked evidence that existed so far was some sort of green and blue fibers they still knew exactly nothing about. She didn't see how that would help. For that matter, would anything?

She looked to the man beside her and reminded herself she still had every reason to be hopeful.

Fowler exited the corridor on the other side of the lobby

and headed their way. Rory sat up straighter, dread swelling in her chest.

"We've got this," Chance said quietly with a glance in her direction.

God, she hoped he was right.

"Sorry to keep you waiting," Fowler said. He looked to Chance.

He stood, thrust out his hand. "Chance Rader from the Colby Agency. I'm a private investigator working with Ms. Harris. Our agency is also handling her defense going forward."

Fowler blinked as if his brain hadn't decided what to spit out in response to the information. After another second or two of hesitation, he shook Chance's hand. The man looked at least a decade older than the last time Rory had seen him. Maybe her case had taken a toll on him. Or maybe the fact that he hadn't done the job as he should have was hanging over his head like a black cloud.

"If you'll follow me," he said without tacking on the please.

Rory rose to her feet, only just realizing she was still seated, and walked alongside Chance. She supposed having to reinvestigate a case was never fun. Never looked good for the detective in charge either. She considered the holes he'd left unaccounted for. The claim that no other prints were found when her brother had been in the cottage and left the food basket. The obliviousness to the fact that it had rained that night. Did they even bother looking for footprints around the house? Certainly none were submitted as evidence. And what about the Taser? Pete had been tased, and no one seemed to have noticed.

Anger bolstered her determination. It was time someone actually tried to find the truth. She and Chance shouldn't have to do it alone. The police had an obligation to at least attempt to do so.

Fowler led them to a room she recognized instantly—the interview room where he had first raked her over the coals.

She stalled at the door. Chance leaned closer. "You okay?"

Big breath. Focus. "Sure." She forced herself to follow the path the detective had taken.

He, of course, sat on the side of the table with his back to the large mirror on the wall. There was a brown folder lying on the table in front of him. As she and Chance took seats on the other side, she wondered who was watching and listening in that observation booth. At the ceiling in the corner beyond that mirror was a camera for the purpose of recording interviews. The red dot indicated it was recording right now.

Didn't matter. She was telling the truth, and she had Chance. As well as the Colby Agency.

Fowler opened the folder, and Rory strained her eyes in an attempt to see what was written on the pages. No luck. The angle prevented her from seeing clearly enough to read the words.

"I just have a few things I want to go over with you, Ms. Harris," Fowler announced.

"All right." She squared her shoulders and lifted her chin. She could just imagine how this was going to go.

"As I'm sure you're aware, we're going back through our previous investigation and looking for anything we may have missed." He gave her a pointed look. "Not that we expect to find anything, but we will do what's required of us."

She said nothing. Hadn't been a question anyway.

He pursed his lips for a moment, studied her closely. "You've had a good deal of vandalism at your house on Tupelo Pike since your release."

That one wasn't a question either. More confusing, she had no idea what his statements so far had to do with her being here.

"It seems to have calmed down now," Chance said when she didn't respond.

His answer was so much better than anything she could have thought to say. Like *that's right, and why aren't you doing something about it?*

"As for the fibers found and not entered into evidence," Fowler said, making Rory sit up and take closer notice, "we're prepared to hand-deliver a sample to the lab of your choice."

"The agency will contact you right away with a location," Chance cut in.

Fowler nodded his understanding. Chance was already texting someone on his phone. Likely Jamie Colby to let her know about this news.

"What is it?" she asked, her nerves going all jittery. "The fibers. I'm sure your lab results speculate as to what the fibers are and where it came from."

"Carpet," Fowler said. "A polyester carpet. Green and blue in color."

Carpet. Rory sifted through the images in her mind for any rugs in the White Cottage. None were green or contained any green as far as she could remember.

"Did the fibers match any in the cottage?" Chance asked.

Fowler shook his head. "The rugs at the crime scene were a shorter nap, and they were wool, not a synthetic."

Fury flamed in Rory's belly. "We had no greenish carpet in our home," she snapped. "Where else would it have come from if not the intruders?"

Fowler held her gaze for a long moment. "For the record, there still is no evidence of an intruder or intruders. And," he held up a hand when she would have blasted him, "it's very possible you picked it up on your clothing from some other location, which is the reason it was not entered into evidence."

Chance spoke before she could. "I'm sure you now understand that the sort of speculation that went into that decision was out of bounds."

Fowler cleared his throat. "At any rate, we're looking into it."

Rory fought to maintain control of her temper. "It rained that night," she snapped. The words popped out of her so unexpectedly and with such fervency, she could only stare at the detective afterward.

He stared right back at her, whether from anger or a lack of what to say next, she couldn't be sure. It was, she realized during the stare-off, astonishing how much older he looked. Gray had completely overtaken his once brown hair. His complexion had grown ruddier, his jowls sagged with visible weariness, and even his suit was rumpled as if worn one too many times between visits to the cleaners. Then again, it was the end of the day. Maybe he was just particularly weary today. Ready for it to end.

Rory was ready for this damned case to end, only the right way this time.

"It did rain, yes." He nodded, the words floating out on a sigh. "But it wasn't enough to wet the ground, which made it irrelevant."

"My feet got wet when I was running for help," she argued.

"But the ground wasn't wet enough to have footsteps make indentations," he argued, "if that's what you're getting at. And—" he looked from her to Chance and back "—for the record, we did look. We just didn't find anything."

Chance spoke up. "Was that before or after the other officers and official personnel were on sight—poking around, obliterating any other tracks?"

If possible, his jowls sagged even lower with the frustration Chance prompted. "We do know how to run an investigation down here, Mr. Rader."

"I'm sure you do," Chance responded. "I am curious, however, as to the reports regarding fingerprints found at the scene. There appears to have been none other than those belonging to Ms. Harris and to the victim."

Fowler rocked his head up and down, the move causing his fleshy neck to waddle. "That's correct."

Rory had to look away. How could he sit there and lie when he must realize they knew he was doing so?

"The basket used to bring the food to the cottage," Chance went on. "Based on the crime scene photos I viewed, it was a natural woven basket with a white lacy cloth inside it. The champagne, a loaf of bread, a variety of cheeses and a few other items that were inside had been removed."

Fowler gave another of those long, slow nods. "That's right."

Chance winced. "You see, that's a problem. Because the newlyweds didn't have the basket with them at the wedding ceremony. Ms. Harris's brother, Austin, picked it up from The Feed Store—where it had been prepared—and took it to the cottage just before the ceremony. He left it on the counter in the kitchen just as it was found when the crime scene photos were taken. His prints as well as anyone at The Feed Store who arranged it should have been on the basket and its contents."

Now the detective's reddish complexion had gone pale. "I'm confident everything in the cottage was checked— even the basket and its contents."

"If the basket is still in evidence," Chance suggested, "perhaps your forensic folks might need to have another look."

The red rushed back into his cheeks with a vengeance.

"There's also," Chance went on when the detective said nothing, "the discrepancy in the autopsy report."

Fowler's forehead folded in bewilderment. "What discrepancy?"

Chance explained about the Taser mark in the photo of Pete's neck. Rory bit her bottom lip. Each time she thought about someone doing that to Pete in addition to everything else, her heart hurt.

Fowler shook his head. "I have no recall of that photo, but rest assured, I will look into it."

Rory barely resisted rolling her eyes. *Fat lot of good that would do.*

Chance smiled when the detective said no more. "Well, if you don't have any other questions, we'll get out of your way. We have some additional interviews to take care of, and I am confident you have a great deal of work to do. My agency will be getting back to you very soon about where to send that overlooked evidence."

He and Rory stood.

The detective scooted back his seat and hefted himself up. "I may need to speak with you again," he said as he made his way to the door.

"Maybe a little more advance notice would help next

time," Chance suggested. "We will likely want the attorney Zoomed in as well."

The detective grunted some indistinguishable response.

Once they were back in the lobby, Rory managed a deep breath. She could not wait to get out of this place. She was certain the police department overall was a good one, but her experience with Fowler and his handling of the investigation into her husband's murder had not been good at all.

"That wasn't so bad," Chance said as they pushed through the exit.

Surprisingly, she had to agree. "Only because you were there."

They were halfway across the parking lot when Rory spotted him.

Anthony Harris. Pete's father was walking toward the double doors they had just exited.

She stalled. Chance stopped to see what she was staring at.

Anthony looked up. His gaze crashed into Rory's.

She didn't know what she expected. Maybe for him to run the other way. Or for him to rush up to her and start screaming—or maybe to start the rant before he even took a step. But he did none of those things. Instead, he continued forward, pausing when he reached her because she had not moved a muscle. She stood motionless like a child in a game of freeze when the music stops. Unlike Eudora, Rory had actually liked Anthony. Even during the investigation and then the speedy trial, he'd remained stoic, not lashing out at her the way Eudora had.

"Rory," he said, then shifted his attention to the man at her side.

"Chance Rader," she explained, startled that her mouth

worked. "From the Colby Agency. He's a private investigator."

Anthony made a sound of acknowledgment. Then he offered his hand. "I suppose you're here to help her figure out where the police fell down on their job."

Chance shook his hand. "I'm here to help her find the truth."

Rory stuck on the comment about the police falling down on their job. He couldn't possibly believe that. He'd been on Eudora's side—firmly against Rory. She had suspected that the police did exactly what the Harrises wanted.

"Well, good luck with finding anything other than what was found before. Which, I'm sure you know, was nothing. No evidence whatsoever to support her story. Believe what you will, but the department did everything in their power to find *all* the facts." He looked at her then. "It's been two years, Rory. Just let it go. Admit what you did and let Eudora and me have some peace."

If he had slugged her, Rory wouldn't have been more aggrieved. She certainly understood that during the trial he had believed she killed his son, but somehow she had hoped that in the nearly two years since, he would have come to see that it wasn't possible.

Clearly, she had hoped for the impossible.

"I told the truth then," she argued, "and I'm telling the truth now. I did not kill Pete. I couldn't have."

When she would have turned away, Anthony took her by the arm. Chance poised to intervene, but she put a hand against his chest to stop him. Let the man say whatever he had to say and get it over with.

"I know you believe that," he urged. "I really do. You were always a good person, Rory, but you made a mistake. You went down a bad path. You can't be sure what you did considering the drug you were on that night. For the life of me, I cannot understand why on earth you felt the need to get high on your wedding night. And why give it to Pete? He never did anything like that in his life. Did you slip it into the champagne?"

Rory barely restrained the tears his words elicited. She gently tugged her arm free of his hold. "I have never done drugs. Not then, not now. The intruders drugged us both. I'm sorry you believe the lies woven by the prosecution."

She walked away, couldn't bear anymore.

They got into Chance's rental car, and she stared forward. She watched Anthony enter the police department. Had he known she was coming and showed up to have his say? If he'd wanted to know what she was up to, Fowler would have kept him informed. Pete's parents got whatever they wanted in this town.

Always had and always would.

But they were not going to win this time. She had not killed Pete, and somehow she was going to prove it.

"You held your own with him," Chance said as he backed out of the parking slot.

"I just told the truth."

Her phone rang. The sound startled her. Shane's name flashed across the screen. She held it up for Chance to see. "It's Shane."

While Chance listened, she answered the call, selecting the speaker option. "Shane?"

"Rory, we need to talk in private."

She glanced at Chance and asked, "Where are you?"

"Meet me at my place. Bring the PI."

"We're heading that way now," she assured him.

The call dropped off.

Chance pulled out of the parking lot. Rory held tightly to her cell phone, her heart pounding. Could Shane share something that changed everything? The better question was, would he?

Carter Residence
Old Larkinsville Road
Scottsboro, 6:45 p.m.

SHANE'S TRUCK WAS in the driveway now.

Chance parked behind it and shifted his attention to Rory. "When he comes to the door, let me go in first. If something feels off, you run back to the car and drive away." He dropped the fob into the cupholder.

"And just leave you here?" She shook her head. "No way."

"I can take care of myself, Rory," he assured her. "Just do this, and I won't have to worry about taking care of you too."

She wanted to be offended, but he was right. She had no real self-defense skills. The only physical fights she had been involved in were in the prison. Both times she'd been pretty banged up. But it happened a lot to the new prisoners. Especially ones like her who appeared privileged. If those doing the beating had only known.

They emerged from the car, walked toward the rickety steps and porch. As soon as they were at the door, it opened. Shane motioned for them to come inside.

Chance walked in first. When he'd had a look around, he gave her a little nod, and she stepped inside as well. She closed the door and steeled herself for whatever was coming next. She didn't want to feel threatened by Shane, but she didn't really trust anyone anymore.

"You'll have to overlook the whole cloak-and-dagger business." He shrugged. "But I feel like things are going to get dicey very soon."

"What do you mean?" Rory asked. She was glad Chance was letting her take the lead with Shane. He might not be as open if the PI, as he'd called him, were the one asking questions.

"You want to sit down?" Shane asked.

She gave him a smile—at least the closest thing to it she could drum up. "Sure."

They settled on his sofa, which looked on the well-worn side but appeared clean. Not like the sofa at Tay Banks's house. Shane dropped into a chair that swiveled. He turned so he could face Rory. The mobile home was old for sure. The paneling was dark, the once white ceiling yellowed. But it was clean. The newer vinyl plank flooring so popular these days shone as if it had been freshly mopped.

"I feel like I was a jerk for not speaking up back then. I suspected things weren't going the way they should with the investigation, but what did I know? I was a rookie. I don't even know if I qualified as a rookie at that point. But like I told you before, now is different. Now I see things and understand."

"What is it," Rory asked then, "that you see?"

"That they're all lying."

"Who is the *they* you mean?" Chance countered.

Rory held her breath, hoped the question wouldn't cause Shane to hesitate.

"Everyone involved in the investigation," he explained without missing a beat. "Fowler. The DA. Your own damn lawyer."

Rory's throat tightened. "What're they lying about?"

Shane cleared his throat, stretched his neck as if needing to buy time. Finally, he said, "There was a case over in Henagar about six months before…what happened to Pete. A couple guys broke into the house where these two women lived—they were a couple, like you and Pete. The perps roughed them up pretty badly." He looked away. "Assaulted one in other ways, if you know what I mean." When he met Rory's gaze, he said, "But nobody died. The perps just did what they did and took a few things of value. A laptop and phones. Some jewelry. Whatever money the women had in the house. Then split."

Rory couldn't speak for a moment. The realization that finally, over two years later, she was hearing this was good news, wasn't it? A shift in the paradigm. She should be overjoyed to learn the crime against her and Pete fit a pattern…except fury roared inside her. Why had no one said anything back then? Before she could launch the rant rising inside her, Chance spoke. "Is there a reason this other case wasn't considered during the initial investigation?"

Shane shrugged. "Sure, but I still think it was a bad call. Since the two women were lesbians, the case was marked as a hate crime. The thinking was that the victims themselves made it different from Pete's murder. No one was killed, and there were actual items of value stolen. Considering all that, it was decided that the other case wasn't related. But I can't get it out of my head that maybe it was."

"Did they catch the perpetrators?" Chance pressed.

Shane scrubbed a hand over his jaw. "I don't know. I haven't thought about that case in over two years."

"Was there a description of the intruders?" Rory suddenly realized why he was so hung up on this case. If the intruders—perps—had looked different from the ones who attacked her and killed Pete, he would have said that, and the other case would have been irrelevant. "They were wearing masks just like the two who came into the cottage, weren't they?"

Shane looked anywhere but at her. "Yeah. They were. Ski masks. Gloves. All black, just like you said about that night."

Rory's lips trembled. "Is there anything else about that case that's similar to mine?"

He shook his head. "Not that I know about."

Chance had his phone out. "I'll need the names of the victims."

Shane provided the names of the two women. "You can google them, and you'll find some information. But not everything. There was a lot that was never released for, you know, the purpose of protecting the investigation."

"But if you could find out this case existed," Rory argued, "anyone could."

"Sure. Like I said, Fowler agreed with the detective who investigated the case in Henagar. It was a hate crime. Not the same thing as what happened to Pete."

Except every cell in Rory's body screamed otherwise.

Chapter Fourteen

Kindred Residence
Tupelo Pike
Scottsboro, 5:00 a.m.

"Rory."

Sleep held her deep in his clutches…there was a dream but she couldn't quite hang on to the pieces of it. Pete was there. Chance too. She was running…

"Rory!"

Her body shook. What was happening?

Arms were suddenly cradling her. "Rory, wake up!"

Her eyes fluttered open. It was dark. Had she imagined the voice…the arms going around her?

"We have to get out of here!"

She tried harder to focus. Chance was holding her in his arms…against his chest. Why was he holding her that way? She coughed…something was wrong.

"…fire!"

Her mind cleared, and the coughing started again. Chance was rushing through the darkness…through the house. There was smoke.

The gold glow of flames snatched her attention. *Fire.* The house was on fire.

She tried to get free. Wiggled against the barriers. Had to run.

"Hang on," he urged, his arms tightening around her.

Suddenly they were outside. Rory didn't remember going through the door…across the porch or down the steps. Chance lowered her feet to the ground. Stuck his cell phone in her hand. "Call 9-1-1."

Then he was gone…*back into the house.*

No. No. That was a bad idea. Her father had gone back into the house…

Rory stood there, unmoving. The image of her father rushing back into their burning home to find her mother expanded in her mind, blocking her ability to do anything but stand there like a statue.

"Chance!" Oh God. What did she do?

Call for help. He'd said she should call 9-1-1. Fingers fumbling, she managed to enter the necessary digits. The dispatcher came on, and Rory spewed out her address and the situation.

The house was on fire. Lulu's house. And Chance was inside.

She dropped the phone and ran for the door. She had to find him. What if he'd succumbed to the smoke? What if he were injured?

Just as she topped the final step to the porch, he burst through the door. Safe. *Not lost and confused in the smoke. Not overcome.*

He ushered her back into the yard, away from the danger.

"I'm sorry." His gaze rested on hers. "It was too out of control by the time I woke up. I couldn't stop it."

She shook her head, her eyes burning from tears or

the smoke or maybe both. "Doesn't matter. We're okay. That's all that matters."

He thrust a white cloth bag at her. "I grabbed a few things for you."

Pillowcase, she realized. She accepted the pillowcase and looked inside. Her cell phone. The photo from her wedding day. The wallet she'd found in her closet and had a few dollars in it. She looked up at him, her body feeling numb…her brain whirling. How did this happen? What did she do now?

Somehow her lips cooperated enough to say, "Thank you."

He dropped his own bag on the ground. The case file was in there. Thank God he'd thought to grab it as well.

Then he put his arms around her and pulled her against him. For a second she wondered why he was hugging her. Not that she minded. His arms felt good. Strong. She needed him…because… She suddenly realized then that she was sobbing.

Lulu's house was on fire. All her things…all the memories…they were lost. Just like her childhood home…her parents…all their things.

Rory wasn't sure how much time passed. She only knew that the thought of withdrawing from this man's arms was more than she could bear at the moment. He was speaking to someone. Sirens were blaring…lights were throbbing.

The fire department had arrived, and she hadn't even noticed. She turned her head, keeping her cheek against his solid chest. They were preparing to put out the flames. The back side of the house was being eaten by the fire. Regret and sadness swelled in her chest. Then she spotted another uniform. The police. Not Fowler. A uniformed officer from Scottsboro PD. Chance was still talking to someone nearby. None of the words made sense to her.

Her knees felt weak. She didn't dare pull away from him.

Movement in her peripheral vision had her lifting her cheek from his warmth. A figure had stepped into view. *Fowler.* He was here too.

Rory drew away from Chance then. Her body swayed, and he steadied her. She refused to look at the house. Instead, she glared at Fowler. Why wasn't he doing his job? If he had done his job when Pete was murdered, none of this would have happened. Damn it. Now everything was gone. Taken from her when she had done nothing wrong. Pete. The home they had shared. Lulu's sweet cottage. Everything.

Except Austin, she reminded herself. She still had her little brother. He too would be devastated by the loss of the home where they had grown up. At the loss of the mementoes that could never be replaced. She glanced back to Chance. Thank God she hadn't lost him.

How had this happened?

Chance was talking to Fowler now. Giving his statement, she assumed.

"The sound of something breaking woke me," he was saying. While he explained this new nightmare, she scanned the ground for his phone. She spotted it and tucked it into the sheet with her things.

Chance had slept in Lulu's room. Rory hadn't wanted him stuck on the couch again. He was kind enough to stay here to ensure she was safe. The least she could do was see to it that he was as comfortable as possible.

She stared at the house…the water now dousing the flames. He had saved her life.

"I sat up on the side of the bed with the intention of getting up to ensure there was no intruder or any new vandalism happening, and I smelled the smoke. I got Rory out of the house and went back in to see if I could get the flames under control, but it was too far gone." He gestured to the pillowcase she carried. "I grabbed a few things and rushed back out."

"Could you see where it started?" Fowler asked. "Appears to be at the back of the house."

Chance nodded. "In the kitchen area."

The kitchen was at the back of the house. Made sense. Whoever did this would want to be behind the house, not in front where someone passing by might see them up to their dirty deeds. By sticking to the kitchen area, no chance of anyone in the bedrooms hearing the heinous work either.

"You should talk to Cade Coleman and Ronnie Smith," she blurted suddenly. "They showed up here that first night when my window was broken. And don't forget about those two who used those paint guns."

Fowler gave her a nod. "I'll talk to them."

Which meant nothing, really. She didn't know why she even bothered. He didn't care if the truth was found when it came to her. The Harris family hated her, and therefore she was nothing. Insignificant.

Fowler moved on to the two uniformed officers on the scene. Another fire department vehicle had arrived, and the man who exited it appeared to be in charge. The fire marshal, she reckoned.

"We can sit in the car," Chance offered.

She didn't really care. No sooner than the thought whizzed through her mind, she realized she was standing in the middle of the yard wearing a nightshirt and with bare feet.

She nodded. "That's a good idea, I guess."

Once they were in the car, she collapsed against the seat and squeezed her eyes shut. Would this nightmare never end? The trouble just kept escalating. When was enough *enough*?

Tears burned in her eyes once more, and she fought them back. She would not cry again. Damn it. Okay. Get it together, Rory. She and Chance had a lot to do. There was no time for falling apart.

A rap on her window made her jump. She sat up and stared at the person on the other side of the glass. *Detective Fowler.* What did he want now? What she wanted was to demand to know why he hadn't brought up the Henagar case when investigating hers...but now wasn't likely the time.

Chance powered the window down.

Fowler looked from Rory to Chance. "You two don't have to stay," he explained. "One of the officers said you'd already answered his questions about any potential items inside that could escalate the situation. I or the fire marshal will contact you if there are more questions."

"Thanks," Chance said before powering the window back up.

When he'd backed out of the driveway and headed toward town, she asked, "What do we do now?"

"First, we're going to get clothes. Then we're going for coffee and food."

She didn't argue. What he suggested was necessary. "What about talking to the people from the case Shane told us about?"

"Heading that way as soon as we're dressed and fed."

"Okay." It wasn't like they could show up at a stranger's home looking like this or at this hour anyway. She glanced at Chance. At least he had on jeans. The tee was one of those sleeveless tanks. The image almost made her smile. He looked like a movie-type tough guy with those muscled arms.

Rory stared forward. She had no idea how this was all going to turn out. But she had the overwhelming urge to laugh. Maybe it was hysteria…insanity…or a combination of both. But she had to bite her lips to prevent the sound from erupting.

How weird was that? Her life just kept unraveling and she wanted to laugh.

Allston Residence
Bray Drive
Henagar, Alabama, 8:15 p.m.

It was probably still too early for a house call from a stranger, but here they were. Chance had parked on the street in front of the home belonging to Alita Whitmore and Carla Allston were both schoolteachers. Rory had searched the internet for as much information as she could find on the two. She just hoped one or both were willing to talk.

Their house was small but very nice. Well maintained. The yard was beautifully groomed with lots of blooming flowers and shrubs. Rory couldn't help thinking of Lulu's home that was now destroyed. Once she'd pulled herself together this morning—about the same time Fowler suggested they didn't have to stay—she had wanted to launch into him about the case with such glaring similarities to hers and Pete's. Shane had told them about it, which meant the local police were not unaware of the case.

But good sense had prevailed. The less Fowler knew about their movements and what they discovered until they were ready for him to know, the better. When they had additional details, then she would throw it at him and demand some answers.

"Ready?" Chance looked to her.

"Yeah. Maybe we'll find out that Shane knew what he was talking about."

"I'm feeling optimistic," Chance noted.

Her too, she decided. Definitely optimistic—in spite of this morning's horror.

As they walked up the sidewalk, a dog barking gave Rory pause. But the sound was coming from inside the house. By the time they reached the steps leading up to the porch, the door had opened.

A woman, mid-thirties maybe, stood there, a small, furry dog clutched in her arms. "Can I help you?"

Chance removed his credentials case from the pocket of his brand-new blue jeans. The cream polo shirt he wore looked good with his tanned skin. It didn't take a lot of imagination to recognize that he would look good in just about anything. She chased away the thoughts. Her mind was tired, obviously. She couldn't stay on track. As for her wardrobe choices, she had selected jeans and a blue pullover. Sneakers and socks. Extra jeans and shirts as well as underthings had been purchased for both of them as well. Chance had swiped his credit card and assured her it was not a problem. She hadn't been shopping in over two years. The prices had surprised her. As long as she stayed out of prison, she would need a whole new wardrobe. And a roof over her head and a job. She felt suddenly exhausted.

But first, she had to get her life back.

"My name is Chance Rader," he was saying to the lady. "I'm from the Colby Agency, and this is Rory Harris. We're looking for Alita Whitmore or Carla Allston. It's about the home invasion that happened about two and a half years ago."

"I'm Alita Whitmore." The woman hesitated a moment. "You're not a cop," she said to him. Then she glanced at Rory. "I know who you are. You're the one who killed your husband."

Rory moistened her lips. "I didn't kill my husband. Two men broke into the place where we were staying. I was raped, and my husband was murdered. I think it may be the same ones who broke into your home. I'm trying to make the police see that there are other cases that could be connected. That's why we're here. I need your help."

The other woman blinked. The hesitation that followed had Rory certain she intended to send them away. Then, "All right. Come in." She moved away from the door, leaving it open for them.

Rory followed, Chance right behind her. The home was nice. Smelled of baked goods. Even after having breakfast, the scent had Rory's stomach sending messages of hunger. It had been so long since she'd been able to enjoy something as simple as the smell of muffins baking or bacon frying. She was so incredibly grateful to have this opportunity—no matter how difficult.

And Chance—she looked at him as he smiled for the woman who had kindly invited them into her home— wouldn't let her down. Not the way everyone else had.

When they were all settled around the living room,

Alita, her dog still cradled against her, looked from Rory to Chance. "How is it you think I can help?"

"Can you tell us," Chance said, "what happened in your case? Start at the beginning, if you don't mind."

Alita was a beautiful woman. Long red hair, green eyes. Her fair skin gave her an ethereal quality. She was short, like Rory, but a little heavier…more muscle than anything else.

"We were home that night. Nothing special about it," she said with a glance at Rory. "We weren't celebrating anything. Just sitting back watching television after dinner. It was kind of late, close to midnight. We'd watched the last three episodes of a series we'd both fallen in love with. It was Friday, so neither of us had to go to work the next morning."

"You're a teacher," Rory said, the thought just now popping in her head. "I'm a teacher as well—was a teacher." She was an ex-con now. The realization sat like a rock in her belly.

Alita nodded. "High school algebra. Carla is a teacher also. Physical education." She laughed. "She keeps me on my toes. We have an entire bedroom devoted to workout equipment." Her smile faded. "But after that night, we took several self-defense classes too. We realized that being strong wasn't enough. We needed to know the weak spots…the places to strike." Her gaze narrowed. "I'd like to see anyone try that crap again."

Rory spoke up then. "I intend to do the same." At least she did if she wasn't sent back to prison.

"You should. Anyway," Alita went on, "we had just decided it was time to go to bed when the back door burst open. Everything suddenly went crazy. Carla and I were screaming. She lunged at one of the intruders, but he knocked her out cold. The other guy grabbed me and dragged me to the bedroom." The fingers of her right hand massaged her dog as if her story had made the animal nervous. More likely she was the one who needed the mindless action.

"Were you drugged?" Chance asked.

At this point, the only details about the case they knew were the ones released to the media, which did not include specifics.

She nodded. "The police called it needle-spiking. They used a typical date rape drug, Rohypnol, but injected it, so it worked faster. Once it kicked in—which was damned fast—my memory gets really foggy."

Chance asked, "Did either of the intruders use a Taser?"

Alita shook her head. "Just the drugs."

So no Taser but the same drugs, injected the same way. At least for Rory. She couldn't be sure about Pete. She'd been told repeatedly that there was no indication of injections on either of them, but she vividly remembered a needle prick. Obviously most of what she had been told was lies.

Rory bit her lip and worked up her courage to ask another of the questions that had stuck in her head. "This may sound like a terrible thing to ask, but did the man who attacked you seem nervous? Shaky?"

Alita frowned, appeared to dig deep for the memory from that awful night. "No. Not that I noticed. Is that how he was with you?"

Rory nodded. "Thinking back, it seems odd."

The other woman shrugged. "Maybe they were in a hurry that night and he was nervous. Here, with me, he was cocky. Forceful, cruel. Over time I've tried to put it behind me…to understand somehow what makes one human want to hurt another so I could get past it. I guess I'm still working on that part."

Rory couldn't see the people who murdered her husband as anything other than monsters.

"Can you describe what either man looked like?" Chance asked.

"I wish. They wore all black. Clothes, shoes, gloves, ski masks. The only thing you could see were their eyes. I remember the guy who grabbed me had gray eyes. Good teeth." She made a harrumphing sound. "But that's it."

Rory's hopes deflated a little. Her attacker's eyes were brown. Did that mean the cases weren't connected after all?

Chance moved on to the next question. "Your partner, Carla, did she remember anything more than you?"

"I know she wouldn't mind me talking to you. She would do about anything to see that both guys involved were caught and got what they deserved. But she had to take her mom to an appointment today, so I'll answer for her. No." She shook her head. "The intruder who grabbed her knocked her unconscious so quickly she didn't have time to take in any details. It was like he didn't care about playing with her the way my assailant did with me. I didn't get a close look at him either before the other guy dragged me into the bedroom." She glanced around. "To be honest, for a long time we weren't sure we could continue living here. We tried to sell the house, but the market was so depressed it never happened. Eventually, we got past it and decided to stay. We repainted the walls. Bought new rugs and replaced about everything they may have touched."

"Did he speak to you?" Rory asked. "Or say anything to the other man?"

She shook her head. "No. They were really careful. It was like they had their routine planned well. They came in, overtook us and did what they'd come to do. There was no discussion, no indecision. Then they were gone."

Rory thought about that for a moment. It was basically the same as what happened at the cottage that night. She hadn't actually considered it in those terms, and the drug had her so in and out, she wasn't completely sure about anything. Maybe not even the color of her attacker's eyes. But the whole invasion seemed to move effortlessly. What little talking occurred had mostly been brief and purposely distorted. Was that just the effect of the drug? Had they worn colored contacts?

She desperately wished she could recall what the shouting was about in the room where Pete was…but she'd faded out. Perhaps it had been her sweet husband begging for mercy…or arguing with the other intruder. The thought hurt her soul.

"What types of items did they take?"

The question Chance asked drew Rory back to the conversation.

"My laptop. The cash in our wallets. Our cell phones. Car keys. Since we had no house phone, we had to go to the closest neighbor's house to call for help."

More of that outrage crept into Rory. The intruders did that to her and Pete as well—took their phones and key fob. Bastards.

"But the most important thing they took," Alita went on, "besides…what they took from us mentally and physically, especially me…was our gold coin collection. Carla inherited that collection from her father. It was worth north of twenty thousand dollars."

Chance and Rory exchanged a glance. That part was

certainly different from what had happened to her and Pete. Of course, they'd had nothing valuable at the cottage—except their lives.

"Was there any mention of similar cases," Chance asked, "that you recall?"

Alita considered his question at length before deciding how to answer. "No." She made a face. "Well, maybe. In the beginning, the detective mentioned another case over in Fort Payne that was very similar. Two men, dressed the same way, came into a couple's home, robbed the place and assaulted the wife, and got out. No one was murdered or injured beyond…well, you know." She seemed to shake herself. "How do you quantify that kind of assault?"

"I understand." Rory wasn't sure when she would ever be ready for sex again. A part of her understood she had to get past that barrier. So far there had been no reason. Maybe there never would be. Her gaze rested on Chance. But there were moments when she felt things with him… so maybe there was hope.

Alita went on, "Carla and I weren't happy when they decided to designate our attack as a hate crime. That's not what it felt like. It felt like two men doing what they wanted to do to two women. I honestly don't think personal beliefs had anything to do with what happened. Frankly, I believe our intrusion was the same as the case in Fort Payne." She turned to Rory. "The murder makes yours different, but there are definitely similarities."

"I've been trying," Rory said, feeling a burst of emotion at the shared travesties, "to get the police to see that there were two men in our cottage that night, and they refuse to believe me because they say there was no evidence. No fingerprints. Nothing to confirm what I said happened."

"Well, obviously, they left no prints because they were

wearing gloves," Alita railed. "The detective on your case should be questioning the guy who assaulted me."

Rory and Chance shared a look. She had to have heard her wrong. "They caught one of your intruders?" How could Rory not know that? Of course she hadn't known. She hadn't even known about the damned case because it was designated as a hate crime.

"Oh yeah," Alita concurred. "He screwed up. Removed his condom while he was still in my bed. He took it with him, but enough semen slipped out onto the sheet for them to get DNA."

"What about the other guy?" Chance asked.

"I guess he was too smart to do something so stupid."

Rory was almost too stunned by the news that there had been an arrest in the case to think, but there was one other thing she had to know. "How long after your attack was he arrested?"

"Months." She grunted a frustrated sound. "Like seven months or so. Rick Hill—that's his name—attacked another woman and was caught in the act. With the DNA evidence from our case, he wasn't getting away. But he never gave up his partner's name. I think they offered him a deal, and he wouldn't take it. The police thought it was someone close to him, but I guess they never could prove it." She exhaled a big breath. "Anyway, we got the locks changed. Had a high-end alarm system with cameras and everything installed. Eventually, we reached the point where we could sleep again."

Chance passed her a business card. "If you think of anything else you believe might help, please give me a call."

"Count on it," Alita promised.

When they were driving away, Rory turned to Chance.

"It makes sense that if the guy wouldn't rat out his partner, it had to be someone close to him, right?"

"It's a strong possibility," he agreed. He braked for a traffic signal. "But if it wasn't, then it means the partner was someone he was afraid of. Someone too dangerous to risk crossing."

And if Rory's gut was right, the unidentified intruder was someone who had done this not just once before, but at least two times. Maybe more. Someone who wasn't afraid of getting caught.

"I'm going to try and get an interview with Rick Hill," Chance said. "I don't know that he will tell us anything, but it won't hurt to try."

"You're right," she agreed. "It can't hurt to try." She leaned back in her seat. "Can we go by the house and see how bad the damage is?"

"We can." He glanced at her. "Then we'll go back to see Detective Fowler. I have a few new questions for him."

Rory studied Chance's profile. "You think we're on to something here. That maybe at least two other cases are related to mine? I mean, there was nothing of real monetary value taken from us." Except the precious life of a good man. "But we weren't home, so there really was nothing to take."

Chance sent a look her way. "I believe there is a strong possibility they are related. But there's one major difference besides the murder."

She waited for him to go on, not daring to breathe.

"The other two we've learned about were home invasions—the homes where the victims lived. Where there was a greater likelihood of finding sellable assets—like that coin collection. There's a possibility they may have targeted the Allston home because of that collection. Your attack didn't occur at your home and didn't appear to be about sellable assets. Which begs the question, were the intruders targeting the place or the two of you?"

The reality of what he had just pinpointed felt like a blow to her gut. He was right. It was no random invasion. Certainly not a random act of violence. It was targeted. Not at the place but at the victims.

This was solid proof! Who couldn't see that? Everyone but her and Chance it seemed.

Kindred Residence
Tupelo Pike
Scottsboro, 10:00 a.m.

THE KITCHEN AREA of the house was a complete disaster. A total loss. That whole section would have to be rebuilt.

The good news was, the other rooms were in pretty good condition other than the smoke and water damage. If Chance hadn't woken up and taken immediate action, the whole house would no doubt have gone up in flames. And they would both be dead.

She glanced at the man walking around the house with her. They weren't allowed to go inside, but Chance had been able to get details from the fire marshal's office. Rory had called Austin and told him the latest episode of their ongoing nightmare. He too was devastated, but also thankful that she was unharmed. He passed along the name of the insurance company Lulu had used. That could wait as far as Rory was concerned. The case was all she could think about right now.

Rory suddenly felt utterly exhausted. She sat down in one of the swings on the old set Lulu had bought second-hand at a moving sale. She'd had to dismantle it and bring it home one piece at a time. In her bug at that. What a sight it was. Another hilarious scene had been Lulu trying to put it back together.

It was a miracle it didn't collapse now with grown-up Rory slumped in one of the swings, but she was too tired to care. On one level, she felt a bit of new confidence given that the case in Henagar was so similar to hers. With potentially another in Fort Payne. There would need to be further investigation—or some way to get the one jailed perp to talk in order to make it matter. The timing appeared to be correct in that he would have still been a free man when it came to the invasion at the cottage. He could very well be the man who assaulted her, except he'd been smarter about not leaving any evidence that time.

She shuddered at the thought.

Either way, she still had no rock-solid proof of the connection.

Chance joined her but didn't risk sitting in the remaining swing. "I think we should try getting another meeting with Carter. He may be able to give us some additional insights since we've spoken with Alita Whitmore. Who knows, he might be able to get us in to talk to the guy they caught, Rick Hill."

Rory tugged her phone from her hip pocket and made the call. It went straight to voicemail. She left a message and ended the call. "Hopefully he'll call me back."

"Next step," Chance said, "I suggest we track down Detective Fowler. I'm sure he'll be thrilled that we're finding more questions for him to answer."

Rory laughed as she rose from the swing. She actually had nothing to laugh about except an image of Fowler hiding under his desk that had just popped into her head. "At least with all these curveballs we keep throwing his way, he won't get bored—as my aunt would say— licking his calf over."

Because he damned sure hadn't done the job right the first time.

Chapter Fifteen

Fowler made them wait a ridiculously long time. While they waited, Chance had dug into the case in Fort Payne via the internet. Again, masked intruders. Again, one victim was sexually assaulted and a number of items were taken. Like the Henagar case, the glaring difference was that no one was murdered.

But the similarities were too great to ignore. Rory was furious no one had seemed to notice or care.

When the detective finally appeared in the lobby, Rory wanted to rant at him. But she kept her cool. Better not to put him on the defensive. He would go there fast enough when Chance threw the first question about the other cases at him.

"Come on back," he said, looking somehow older and wearier than he had this morning.

Rory had no sympathy. She was tired too. If he had done his job the right way two years ago, they wouldn't be here right now.

This time he led them to an actual office. Maybe he'd

gotten a promotion, or he'd borrowed someone else's space. At least they weren't in that awful interview room. Many of her nightmares over the years had revolved around that room where the detective had tried every possible tactic in his playbook to make her confess.

When they had all taken seats, he regarded first Rory, then Chance. "If you're looking for answers about the house, you'll have to wait until I have the report from the fire marshal. Right now, you know as much as I do."

"We're here," Chance said, "about the Whitmore and Allston case."

Fowler exhaled a big breath. "That case was not the same as yours," he said to Rory. Then, turning back to Chance, he continued, "the cases were different. If you did your research, you know the one in Henagar was primarily a hate crime."

"The man who was caught and charged," Chance countered, "Rick Hill, where was he imprisoned?"

"Limestone Correctional Facility. I only tell you this because I know how easy it is for you to find out on the internet. And because," he turned to Rory again, "going to see the perv involved is a waste of time."

"It's possible that it will be a waste of time," Rory agreed, frustration and anger building inside her way too fast. "The two intruders in that case may or may not have targeted the victims specifically. It may have been about the coin collection they stole."

"Don't forget the hate crime part," Fowler growled.

"Which means," Chance interjected, "that Rory and her husband were likely the targets rather than anything they may have had in their possession at a rented house."

Before Fowler could find whatever he wanted to say next, Rory pressed on, "There was another very similar case in Fort Payne just five months before the one in Henagar. Again, one victim was sexually assaulted. Both were drugged and things were stolen."

Why did the man not see the similarities? The obvious connection!

"But," Fowler argued, "as you have already discovered, there was significant property stolen in both." His gaze settled on Rory. "If—big, fat if—there was even any evidence someone else came into that cottage the way you suggest, the only items taken were your cell phones and car fob—but not the car. A very different scenario. And we all are acutely aware that there was no evidence to support your claim."

"What evidence was found in the other two cases?" Rory demanded, her anger building. "No prints for sure. The DNA you were able to retrieve at the Henagar home was an accident. If that one thing hadn't been found, would you have insisted nothing happened there either? That there were no intruders? That the victims stole their own stuff?"

Fowler glared at her, his mouth shut tight.

"Perhaps what you're not taking into consideration," Chance said, "is that the Harris case was meant to look that way—different from the others. Because the White Cottage attack was not about property but about the people there that night."

Fowler shook his head. "Mr. Rader, I can appreciate how this all looks to you and to Rory. But we went over all that. I interviewed Rick Hill myself—twice. He knew nothing about the Harris case. You're both ignoring the most glaring difference in the other cases. *No one was murdered.* And there was no supporting evidence whatsoever in your case," he railed at Rory. "Both of the other homes showed obvious signs of breaking and entering. Both had been ransacked. There were footprints found at one. Bodily fluids at the other. There was no—let me repeat, *no*—evidence at yours."

"There's this thing," Rory snapped, "called escalation." She and Chance had discussed the term and its meaning in cases like this. "Someone died in my case and then the two intruders backed off their crime spree. In the attack where Hill was caught, he was working alone. Things had changed maybe because of that escalation."

"Not to mention," Chance said, "even if we set aside the possibility that Pete and Rory Harris may have been targeted, most repeat offenders learn from their previous mistakes. When they broke into the cottage where Rory and her husband were staying, they had at least two events to their credit. So they made sure there was no sign of breaking and entering and no evidence left behind. The murder was likely because one of the two got carried away—escalated—then the team split apart. Hasn't that been your experience over your lengthy career, Detective? Criminals often escalate. Those working together often go their separate ways."

"I suspect," Fowler countered, ignoring Chance's question, "the backing off was about one of the intruders being caught and—"

"Which didn't happen," Chance cut him off, "until after the attack on Rory and her husband. And only then because he attempted to assault another woman whose boyfriend came home just in time."

"As I said," Fowler repeated, "I interviewed Hill myself. He and the partner he refused to identify had nothing to do with the Harris case. We know what happened in the Harris case." He set his gaze on Rory. "The only evidence in the whole place showed us what happened."

Renewed fury roared through her. He would not be swayed. They were wasting their time. He intended for her to go back to prison whether she had committed murder or not.

"You're saying," Chance argued, "that Hill had an alibi."

"He did. I confirmed it just to rule out exactly this. Someone coming along trying to tie that case to the Harris case." He shook his head, his expression lifting a little with the triumph he felt. "No connection whatsoever. No evidence that anyone other than Pete Harris and his new wife were in that cottage."

"What about the unidentified partner?" Chance asked. "Did he have an alibi too?"

"As if I could know that." Fowler threw up his hands in mock surrender. "I can see that I'm not going to be able to convince you."

"What about the unidentified fibers?" Chance tossed out. "Any more theories on that evidence you did find at the cottage?"

"We've talked about that already, Mr. Rader," Fowler tossed back. "There's nothing new related to the carpet fibers Rory or her husband could have picked up anywhere."

"So you're not going to listen," Rory accused. "Exactly like before. You never followed through. Just accepted that I killed my husband when I had zero reason to want to hurt him. For God's sake, what was my motive?" She wanted to shake him. To scream. But it would do no good.

His gaze bored into Rory's. "Drugs can do that, Ms. Harris."

She stood, unable to listen to any more.

Chance stood as well. "Appreciate your time, Detective," he said before following Rory from the office.

She stormed out of the building, away from the department that had let her down so completely when her husband was murdered and would no doubt do it again. Pete deserved justice, by God. She climbed into the passenger seat of the car and steamed.

The anger suddenly gave way to defeat and regret and so many other emotions she could barely hold back the tears.

When Chance slid into the driver's seat, she turned to him, her soul aching. "I need to go to the cemetery. I haven't been there since I got home." She needed to be close to Pete for a minute.

He nodded. "I'll take you there now."

Rory sank deeper into the seat. She was so tired of fighting a losing battle. So disgusted with the lack of support from anyone except Chance and the Colby Agency. With effort she steadied her resolve. She could not give up. Not until she found the truth and the people responsible for her husband's murder were behind bars.

She suddenly wondered whether, she sat face-to-face with the man who assaulted her, she would recognize him. The one in Limestone Correctional Facility was the one who assaulted Alita Whitmore and the woman in Fort Payne. He could be the one.

"Are we going to that prison?" She looked to the man driving. If anyone could get her in to see that scumbag, it was Chance.

"We're going to try."

The thought filled her with sudden uncertainty. If they were right, Hill could hold all the answers. If they were wrong…then they were back to square one, and there was nothing in square one.

The notion of starting over was a physical pain in her being.

Either way, she had no choice but to continue. If she failed, she would undoubtedly be going back to prison. She couldn't find the truth there…she couldn't go back. Did the truth no longer matter to anyone but her?

How could Pete's parents believe she had killed him? Why didn't they at least want to look into the alternative? To be certain.

More painful to consider, why would anyone want to hurt her or Pete? If Chance was right, and she felt sure he was, what had she or Pete done to warrant murder? Right now, there appeared to be no other motive for what happened.

Which left only the conclusion that maybe Pete was the target since he was murdered and she was left alive. Whether for something he knew or had done or possessed or just to punish Rory. She had to find that truth.

But Louis Larson insisted there were no business issues at the time. Was it possible her husband had a terrible secret Rory didn't know about?

She didn't want to believe such a thing. Determination soared through her. She would not believe it. Not until she had no other choice.

Cedar Hill Cemetery
Cedar Hill Drive
Scottsboro, 1:00 p.m.

RORY KNELT NEXT to her husband's grave and traced the words engraved on his black granite headstone. Beloved

Husband and Son. The ache in her chest made her lips tremble. How had it been more than two years since she had stood right here and sobbed like a baby over this sweet man as his coffin was lowered into the ground?

Chance knelt next to her. "It's a beautiful place."

It was. Pete's parents had bought plots in this cemetery long ago when the most beautiful locations were still available. The branches of the grand old tree that stood nearby reached across Pete's grave, lending shade in the long, hot Alabama summers. The bench beneath the tree had been added by his parents. She'd expected to come here often and visit, but that hadn't happened because she had been in prison.

"They wanted him buried here." She sat on the backs of her calves, suddenly too tired to hold herself up. "I never considered the ramifications. This is a single plot. Their double plot is on the other side of the tree. They wouldn't have wanted me buried next to him if I had died too." She laughed sadly. "I'm not sure what poor Austin and Lulu would have done with me."

To occupy her hands, she reached out and pulled away a random weed from the base of Pete's headstone. There were no flowers. His birthday would be coming up next month. She should get flowers. Eudora no doubt would. If she saw flowers from Rory, she would likely throw them away. Rory would need to put hers out early.

How could the woman not have seen how very much Rory had loved her son?

"Let me take you to lunch," Chance offered. "Then we can stop by a floral shop and pick up flowers if you'd like."

She turned to him, surprised that he would think of such a kind gesture. "I would love that. Thank you."

His smile was so kind, so handsome. How had she

been so lucky to have this man as the one to help her right this wrong?

"Besides your brother," he said, "it's been a long time since anyone was nice to you. You deserve someone to be nice to you."

Her lips lifted in a smile of her own. "I'm so glad the Colby Agency sent you."

His fingers curled around her hand. "Me too."

He stood, pulled her up with him. "How about we go to that drugstore where you had your first job?"

"They have great milkshakes too."

"Chocolate, right?"

"Always."

Rory glanced one last time at Pete's headstone. If she could do nothing else, she hoped she could make sure the person who did this to him was brought to justice.

The thought nudged her. "I've been thinking," she said as they walked through the cemetery to where Chance had parked his car. "I figure whoever set fire to my house was someone like the guys who broke my window or used the paint guns. But what if it wasn't?"

They paused next to the car. "You mean, what if it was the person who killed your husband?"

She nodded. "Maybe he was cool, going on with his life as long as I was in prison, but he could be getting nervous now."

"I've considered that possibility," Chance agreed. "Which is all the more reason not to let you out of my sight for an instant going forward."

"Where will we stay?" They certainly couldn't go back to her house.

"I still have that room. We could go there or another place if you prefer."

"I'm good with whatever you think." *As long as I'm with you*, she kept to herself.

She felt safe with Chance. She felt happy…in a tiny, unexpected way.

Chapter Sixteen

Limestone Correctional Facility
Nick Davis Road
Harvest, Alabama, 3:45 p.m.

Chance wasn't surprised in the least that Alfred Mannington, the agency attorney assigned to Rory's case, had come through quickly. Chance had made the call as they left the cemetery, and before two o'clock, they'd had approval for a visit to Rick Hill at the prison.

Chance had also taken Rory to a floral shop and then back to the cemetery. From there they had driven straight to the prison.

They'd been brought to a private visitation room. Rory looked nervous, but Chance felt she was holding up as well as could be expected under the circumstances. She had been through a lot.

The fire and subsequent destruction at her aunt's home had been a painful blow. He wished he could have stopped the progress of the flames without the necessary water damage caused by the fire department. But there had been no choice. Added to that, the confirmation that Detective Fowler for some reason refused to even consider the other two cases as being connected to Rory's was infuriating. Made for a bad day.

Chance would not stop until he found the connection or the person who had murdered Pete Harris.

The idea that the lowlife they were about to interview was possibly the man who had assaulted Rory twisted in his gut. On the long drive here, he had mentally prepared himself for the necessity of sitting across a table from her attacker without reaching for this throat. Not exactly the sort of thing that helped get answers for their questions.

"You think he'll tell us anything?"

Rory's question tugged Chance back to the moment. "We can hope. He received a life sentence without the possibility of parole. It's not like he has a whole lot to lose."

Then again, Alabama was one of the states that still had the death penalty.

The door opened. Rory stiffened, her tension escalating. Chance wished there was more he could say to relieve that tension, but that would be impossible. If this man was the one…

He blocked the thought. Needed to focus.

Rick Hill was forty. He'd celebrated his recent birthday behind bars. This wasn't his first time behind bars. He had a lengthy rap sheet. Mostly low-level brushes with the law, but he'd screwed up royally that last time. The last two times, in fact. First by leaving his DNA at a crime scene and then by getting caught in the transmission of a crime.

The guards ushered Hill to the chair on the other side of the table. His wrists and ankles were shackled. One of the guards fastened the shackles to the hook latch bolted to the floor.

"Let us know when the interview is over," the taller of the two guards said just before they exited the room.

Chance's attention settled on the prisoner then. Hill's hair was buzzed short. The gray eyes that Alita Whitmore had mentioned shifted from Chance to Rory.

Fury tightened Chance's lips, but he forced himself to relax. What he needed from this bastard—all he needed—was the name of his partner. The one who likely murdered Pete Harris.

"Mr. Hill," Chance said, drawing the man's attention back to him.

"That's me," Hill said as if Chance had asked a question.

"You and a partner," Chance began, "broke into the home of Alita Whitmore and Carla Allston on December 20, year before last."

He made a rude sound and rolled his eyes. "What of it?"

"The two of you drugged your victims and took a number of items from their home."

"Look." He set his gaze on Chance, a smirk on his face. "If you're here to ask about those gold coins, I got no clue what he did with them. He gave me cash for my share, and that's all I can tell you."

"What the two of you did with the items you stole is irrelevant to me, Mr. Hill."

Another roll of his eyes. "*Irrelevant*," he mocked in a squeaky voice.

"Did you kill my husband?" Rory demanded abruptly.

Dead silence lingered for about five seconds. Chance waited, watched the man's reaction.

His gaze swung to Rory, and he stared.

Chance fought the urge to rail at him or punch the hell out of him.

"Why would I kill your husband? I don't even know

you." He made a face and looked away, stared at the wall as if something interesting was there that only he could see.

"Pete Harris was my husband. You and your partner came into White Cottage on our wedding night and murdered him and raped me. So don't pretend you don't know him or me."

He turned his face back to Rory. Another smirk appeared. "I think I would remember if I had ever been inside you."

Chance leaned forward, the urge to act pulsating in his veins. "You should watch your mouth."

Hill laughed. "What you gonna do? Beat me up?" He shook his head. "Get over yourself, hotshot. Besides, she started it."

Beneath the table, Rory rested a hand on Chance's thigh.

Chance drew back, regained some semblance of control—at least with his anger. Her touch had him feeling other things he shouldn't. "Just answer the lady's question, Hill."

The scumbag exhaled an exaggerated breath. "I ain't never set out to kill no one." He looked directly at Rory then. "And I didn't touch you."

His non-answer to the murder of Pete Harris was not lost on Chance. "Why did you let your partner screw you over?"

"What makes you think I did?" the man in prison garb countered.

"Because you're the one sitting here," Chance fired back.

"What can I say?" He shrugged, the jumpsuit baggy

on his shoulders. "I screwed up. Advice from the wise, pal. Never remove a condom too soon. Stupid mistake."

"Then your partner," Rory said, her voice shaking a little, "the one you're protecting, killed my husband."

A grin spread across his face. "No, he was a little busy…if you know what I mean."

Chance stilled. Now they were getting somewhere. The cocky bastard had just allowed something to slip. It might not be actual evidence, but it was enough for Chance to understand they were going in the right direction.

To Rory's credit, she held her ground. Didn't draw away or show any fear. "Then you're the one who killed my husband."

Shock appeared on the scumbag's face as if he'd just realized what he'd done. "You're crazy." He looked to Chance. "You should take her home. She needs her meds."

"She's right," Chance reiterated. "If you weren't the one who attacked her, then you were with her husband, which makes you his killer."

Hill scoffed. "I wasn't even there. That was somebody else's job. Not ours. Or—" he cocked his head and stared at Rory "—you killed him. After all, y'all had just got married. Didn't the rich boy have insurance?"

That was the thing. The insurance didn't matter. If the beneficiary was convicted of murdering the insured, the payoff went to the next legal beneficiary. In this case, the parents.

"What did you do with his Rolex and wedding ring?" Chance tossed out.

• "What the hell you talking about?" Hill snarled. "That bastard wasn't wearing a Rolex, and the wedding band was just plain old…" He snapped his mouth shut.

Chance smiled. *Gotcha.* This guy really was stupid. Not to mention gullible.

"It was you," Rory said, the words barely a whisper of breath.

"I'm done here," Hill shouted, rattling his shackles.

"We know what you did," Chance warned as he leaned closer. "But we're not here for you. We want the other guy."

He'd fallen for a trick once. Chance could only hope he'd fall for this one as well.

Hill glared at him for a long moment. "You can't touch him," he hissed, low as if he feared the walls could hear.

"No one," Chance argued, "is untouchable."

The bastard laughed then, long and loud with his head thrown back.

Chance and Rory shared another look. The hurt in hers almost undid him. Made him want to leap across the table and tear this lowlife apart.

Finally, Hill rested his gaze back on Chance. He leaned forward and whispered, "He's untouchable, man. *Protected.* Trust me on that one."

Chance narrowed his gaze, scrutinized the other man's face. Every instinct said he was very likely telling the truth. "I thought you were the one," he whispered. "The one who liked having that extra bit of fun."

Hill sneered and leaned closer. "Since I know you or they—" he glanced at the camera on the wall "—can't record this or use it if they do, I will tell you this much. Fact is, he wouldn't let me have *her*," he whispered and glanced at Rory, waggled his eyebrows. "He wanted her for himself." He shifted his sleazy gaze back on Chance. "And I got stuck with the rich boy. I guess I got a little excited watching him beg us not to hurt her." He leaned closer still. "He. Just. Wouldn't. Shut. Up. The Taser didn't even shut him up."

Rory shot up from her chair and rushed away from the table. She banged on the door. Shouted for the guard.

Hill grinned. "I sure wish I had gotten that one."

Chance barely restrained the urge to beat his stinking face to a pulp. Instead, he stood, leaned over the table. "Thanks for your help. I'll be sure to tell your partner how you outed him."

Hill's grin slipped. "I didn't tell you nothing."

Chance was the one who laughed then. "Actually, you did. I know exactly who you're talking about."

As the guard opened the door and they exited, Hill shouted profanities, ending with a warning.

"Go ahead, tell him whatever you want…but all you'll get is dead."

Chapter Seventeen

Corner Motel
Tupelo Pike
Scottsboro, 6:30 p.m.

Rory paced the floor of the small room. On the way back from the prison, she and Chance had discussed at length every horrible thing Rick Hill had told them. Particularly the last part when he'd inadvertently confessed to killing Pete.

What he'd said wouldn't hold up in court, since it would be their word against his. But she knew. She had understood him perfectly.

Chance had started reviewing the case file as soon as they arrived back at the room. The conclusions he had thrown out to her were looking more and more on the money. This whole business about the other man—the one who assaulted her—being protected had to mean he was…maybe…probably a cop.

She stalled, turned to the desk where Chance sat with the file spread out in front of him. "You really think it could be Shane?" Now that she thought about it, he did have brown eyes. She exhaled a weary breath. But so did millions of other people. Brown was the most common eye color.

Putting aside what had been done to her…the idea she was mentally tossing around would mean that Shane knew who killed Pete! He had been there when it happened and done nothing. Told no one.

"It's possible," Chance agreed. "He would fit the profile as someone protected in Hill's eyes since he's a cop. He could be in a position to manipulate evidence. He would know how to clean up a crime scene…how to ensure he wasn't caught."

Rory considered what she knew about Shane. "His mother was Mr. Harris's younger sister. I remember Pete mentioning that she didn't do very well for herself. Married some drug dealer who ended up going to prison. She and Shane had a difficult time. I think Pete's dad helped them out, but Eudora wasn't happy about it. Mrs. Carter died, overdosed, and Shane ended up going into police work."

"He was a traffic cop with the city," Chance said. "The deputy position came along right around the same time Pete was murdered."

The thought that he was the protected one—that he had hidden the identity of Pete's killer—made her sick. Even worse, unless Shane confessed, there was nothing they could do to prove any of this. Rick Hill certainly wasn't going to own a murder rap and risk being sentenced to the death penalty.

Rory turned to Chance. Defeat sucked the certainty out of her. "There's nothing we can do."

Chance looked down at the pages spread across the desk. "I say—" he looked to her then "—we have a go at Carter. See what he has to say for himself."

Could she do that? Could she stand face-to-face with Shane and not lose it?

She had tried calling him twice since they left the prison. He hadn't answered or called back. That left only one option. Find him and confront him. Yes, she could do it. She had to. It was imperative if she was ever going to find the truth. If he was innocent in all this...then he shouldn't have a problem talking to them. For God's sake, he was the one who told them about the Henagar case!

Deep breath. Guilt drove people to do strange things.

Part of her hoped he was innocent...she had never had any reason to dislike Shane. But if he was the one and, dear God, it sure seemed possible, she would see to it that he...what? She couldn't force him to confess. She couldn't produce evidence that did not exist.

"I'm ready," she said to Chance.

She needed to remember that she was no longer in this alone. The Colby Agency would help her get to the truth. Look how far they had come already in just two days.

Carter Residence
Old Larkinsville Road
Scottsboro, 7:00 p.m.

RORY'S NERVES STARTED to tangle when Chance pulled into Shane's driveway. His truck was there. Surely that meant he was home.

She climbed out of the car, surveyed the area. It would be dark in another hour. The gloom was already setting in. On the drive over, she had kept trying to recall the moments when her attacker had been on top of her that night. But the drug had held her firmly in its grip. She knew he'd been strong and that he had brown eyes.

And that he seemed nervous. His body seemed to tremble or shiver.

She shuddered at the thought. Hugged her arms around herself.

When they reached the steps that led to the porch, Chance hesitated. He turned to Rory. "The door is open."

Her gaze shot to the door. It was partially open. Fear snaked up her spine. "Shane!" she shouted. "You home?"

Chance started up the steps. He held up a hand when she would have followed. He shook his head. Instead, she reached into her pocket and withdrew her cell phone, ready to call for help if there was trouble.

Could Rick Hill have managed a phone call to warn Shane?

Her heart thundered so hard in her chest she felt as if it might burst. Could he have taken off? If he had, they might never find him…might never be able to confirm the truth.

Chance pushed the door open wider. "Carter, you here?"

Rory held her breath as Chance disappeared into the trailer. What if Shane had gotten a call, and he'd rushed home to grab a few things before taking off? What if he had seen them pull up and was waiting to ambush Chance?

She rushed up the steps and through the door.

Then she froze.

Shane lay on his side on the kitchen floor, his back to her. She couldn't see any blood. Had he fallen and hit his head? Passed out from some sort of medical episode?

"Is he okay?"

Chance walked around Shane and lowered into a crouch next to him. When he looked up at her, his face was grim. "He's dead."

Rory's knees nearly buckled. Bile burned her throat. "How…" She swallowed at the tightness in her throat. "How did he die?"

Chance stood. "Stabbed."

She dared to step closer and see for herself. The knife was large…like the bigger one found in those knife block sets. A quick survey of the counter confirmed her assumption. The block, one slot empty, stood ominously next to the sink.

Shane had been their last hope to find the truth. Now he was dead. How in the world would they ever make Fowler see how wrong he had been? She stared at the man she had known as shy and nice. Who would have killed him? His partner in crime, Hill, was sitting in prison.

"Rory."

Chance's voice sifted through the haze of disbelief and defeat shrouding her brain. She turned to him.

"We should go outside and call this in."

She blinked. Another question suddenly overriding all else. "How long has he been dead?"

"Not long." Chance nodded to the man on the floor. "The blood hasn't even coagulated. His skin is still fairly warm. We need to get outside."

Rory got it. They were contaminating a crime scene.

Once they were outside, leaving the door ajar just as it had been, Chance ushered her toward the rental car. He called 9-1-1. Rory stood next to the passenger door, her arms once again around her body.

Shane was dead…but was there evidence somewhere inside that could prove he had lied? That he had been at White Cottage the night Pete was murdered?

Would the police cover up any evidence they found inside now?

She had to go back in there and look.

When she started forward, Chance stopped her. "You can't go back in there, Rory. The police will be here soon, and—"

She glared at him. "There could be evidence in there. Something that proves what he did."

Chance nodded. "I know, but we can't go back in. It's too risky. We're already going to be viewed as persons of interest just because we're here."

She wilted. "They'll hide the truth…just like before."

He put his arm around her and pulled her close. "We won't let them hide anything this time."

Scottsboro Police Department
South Broad Street
Scottsboro, 9:00 p.m.

FOWLER HAD QUESTIONED her extensively, and every word had dripped with accusation.

He saw her as his prime suspect.

Rory wanted to scream. It had been after eight before she was brought here. Chance had been allowed to drive his car, but one of the deputies who showed up at Shane's trailer had brought her in. She'd expected to be taken to the sheriff's department, but she'd been brought to Fowler's office instead. He'd explained that the homicide was part of his ongoing investigation.

His first words to Rory had been: *"Do you really think you can murder your way out of this?"*

He obviously truly believed she was guilty. That she had murdered her husband and was now desperately trying to prove her innocence by whatever means necessary. Unbelievable.

Maybe there was a way to find out if Rick Hill had called Shane or someone else. The thought was a foolish one. Still, she knew better than most how some prisoners managed to get their hands on burner phones. No one would ever know if and to whom he might have made that call. The realization that Rick Hill was the only remaining witness who could prove what really happened in the cottage that night terrified her.

If he ended up dead…she would never be able to prove she was telling the truth.

She glanced at the doors that led down the corridor where Fowler's office was. Once he'd taken Chance back for questioning, she had been sequestered to the lobby. It wasn't like she was going anywhere unless she wanted to walk in the dark. There was no one for her to call. All her friends had abandoned her. Austin was in Nashville, and she wasn't ready to call him yet. There was nothing he could do anyway.

Besides, she wasn't going anywhere until Fowler was finished questioning Chance.

Rory drew in a big breath and slumped in her chair. She was so tired of butting this brick wall. She closed her eyes. If not for Chance and the Colby Agency, she would likely be charged with Shane's murder already. Chance was the only reason she had gotten this far. She worried that at this point, it would take a miracle to ever make anyone see she had not killed her husband.

"Rory."

Her eyes flew open, and she peered up at the voice. Anthony Harris stood over her. For a moment, she felt so disoriented she couldn't speak.

Where had he come from? What was he doing here? Why was he talking to her? The man had turned his back on her just as his wife had…just as nearly every-one else had.

"I just heard about Shane."

She blinked. The idea that she was not hallucinating finally sank in. She moistened her lips, found her voice. "He was murdered." A sharp intake of air made her real-ize she'd stopped breathing the moment he said her name. "Stabbed…like Pete."

"We need to talk." Anthony glanced around the nearly deserted lobby. "Can you spare a few minutes?"

Somehow she levered herself to her feet. "Of course. What would you like to talk about?" Dumb question but a necessary one.

"Let's step outside." He looked around again, his gaze hesitating on the officer at the desk and a couple of other uniforms nearby.

"All right."

She moved into step next to him as they crossed the lobby. He held the door for her to go outside ahead of him. Once they were clear of the entrance, he gestured to his vehicle.

"We can sit in my SUV."

It was the same big, black SUV he'd owned when she and Pete met. One of the most expensive models.

Once they were inside the vehicle, it was as if the world had gone silent. The luxurious SUV was nearly sound-proof.

Anthony sat facing forward, his hands braced on the steering wheel. Rory waited for him to speak. She had no clue what he wanted to say, but she wasn't about to shat-ter the moment by speaking. One wrong word from her could suddenly stop his abrupt about-face.

She wondered if Eudora knew he was here.

She stared forward as well. Wished Chance would appear in the lobby. She should send him a text to let him know what she was doing. She started to reach for her phone, and the man spoke.

"I believe Shane had something to do with Pete's murder."

For a moment she felt sure she had heard him wrong. "What?"

He nodded. "I'm almost certain it was him." His head swiveled so that he faced in her direction. "I thought he acted funny at the funeral. Then he disappeared for training. It just all seemed so coincidental."

She held back the anticipation, too afraid to get her hopes up yet. "Do you have any kind of proof?"

He looked her squarely in the eye then. "I do. Yes. I wasn't sure until your conviction was overturned and we learned there would have to be a new trial. That made me take a long hard look at everything. I started to think about all the little things that didn't add up."

Despite her throat being nearly closed, she managed to swallow. "What little things?"

"Like I said, how he behaved at the funeral. Then he withdrew from our lives. I can't even tell you the last time I saw him until yesterday."

"You saw him yesterday?" He'd met with Shane yesterday, and now he was here with her. That had to mean something. Had Anthony confronted him? Was he going to share whatever he believed with her now?

He looked at her again. "There's something you need to see."

"Okay."

He started the SUV and backed out of the parking slot. About half a dozen emotions turned on inside her.

Hope…fear…uncertainty. But determination won the battle. Rather than demand to know where he was taking her, she sat back, buckled her seat belt and let him drive.

They rode across town in silence. All the shops were closed. Only a restaurant here and there remained open. The idea that she was hungry flitted through her mind. But all that mattered right now was that maybe she was about to learn the truth.

He turned on the blinker and took the right onto Old Larkinsville Road.

"Are we going to Shane's house?"

Anthony didn't answer. Just stared straight ahead and kept driving.

The fear took top billing then. "I should let Chance know. He's probably looking for me by now." She pulled out her cell phone.

Anthony snatched it from her hand.

She tried to reach for it. "What're you doing?"

His window rolled down, and he tossed her phone out.

Oh hell. "Stop this car and let me out now." She reached for the door handle then.

The gun was in her face before she could blink.

Pete's father had a gun?

The realization startled her. Pete insisted his family hated guns. He hated guns.

Even in the dim glow from the dash lights, she could see that this was no little gun either. It was bigger…like the ones the thugs in the movies carried.

Her heart started that crazy wild pounding again. She glanced around the vehicle. The console. The dash. Where was Anthony's cell phone? Probably in his pocket. She stared at the jacket he wore. He and Pete had been alike in the way they dressed. Always neat and professional. Even in the summer they wore lightweight sports jackets.

God, she missed him.

She had to think…had to find a way to pull this situation back.

"You're right," she said in hopes of shifting his attention from the gun he held in one hand while he navigated the SUV with the other. "I think Shane was involved in Pete's murder."

Anthony said nothing.

"Rick Hill, the man who worked with him on those other robberies, told us that we would never be able to pin anything on Shane because he was untouchable."

Anthony still said nothing, but his jaw visibly tightened.

She was making headway. "Shane himself told me he knew I was innocent." That was a stretch, but Anthony didn't know.

His foot seemed to press harder on the accelerator with every word she said. The way he took the curves had her stomach pitching. But she couldn't stop. She had to make him see that whatever he was thinking, he was wrong about her.

"I would never have hurt Pete," she said, struggling to sound calm and reasonable. "I loved him, and he loved me. How do you think he would feel, knowing his family had treated me this way?"

"You—" he glared at her, taking his eyes from the road "—don't bring my son into this."

The wheels bounced off the edge of the pavement, and he whipped the steering wheel left to get back fully on the road. Regaining control of the vehicle required both hands. At least the gun wasn't aimed at her anymore.

Rory's seat belt tightened on her shoulder. Her pulse skittered into panic mode. He was going to get them both killed. "Please slow down."

The speed lessened a fraction.

"I know you think I did this awful thing," she said, defeat weighing on her. "I get it. But you're wrong. I truly believe it was Shane and that…awful Rick Hill."

"Just shut up," he snarled.

"Mr. Harris," she urged, "whatever you think of me, consider your wife for a moment. Eudora needs you. If you do this…whatever it is you have in mind…she's going to be devastated."

"Everything I have ever done," he spewed, "was for her."

The headlights flashed over the trailer in the distance. Shane's house. The police were gone now, but yellow crime scene tape was draped around the place. Hanging ominously from the trees around his yard.

Anthony turned into the driveway. Shane's truck was gone. She imagined the police had taken it to a lab for inspection.

The man behind the wheel got out. Her fingers closed around the door handle, but if she tried to run, he would just shoot her. She couldn't outrun a bullet. Especially since she had no idea what sort of marksman he was.

Anthony came around to her door. He jerked it open. "Get out."

Since the gun was aimed at her once more, she did as he said.

"Go inside," he ordered.

She walked the few feet to the porch steps and climbed them slowly. She stood at the door, but it was sealed shut.

The mobile home was a crime scene. The police tape on the door left no doubt.

"Open it."

She started to argue but didn't see the point. Instead, she twisted the knob and pulled with all her might. Didn't budge.

"It's locked."

He shoved her to the side, then used his whole body to force the door open. Again, Rory glanced around and wondered what her odds were of getting out of his line of sight before he could shoot.

Just then he grabbed her by the arm and forced her inside. He flipped on a light.

The stench of blood hung in the air. Rory figured it had been too fresh when she and Chance had arrived, or maybe it was worse now just because she knew what had happened.

"Why are we here, Anthony?" She looked to the man who held the gun. In his face were glimpses of Pete. He'd looked far more like his father than his mother. He'd barely inherited anything from her, in Rory's opinion. He'd been kind and slow to anger like his father. She stared at the gun in Anthony's hand. Had his son's murder driven him to this?

"You did all this," he said.

She wanted to argue with him, but it didn't seem prudent. He had a gun, after all. Surely Chance was out of his interview by now. Would one of the officers in the lobby recall who she'd left with? Were there cameras that would show her leaving?

"It was your fault." He squeezed his eyes shut as if the need to cry had suddenly overwhelmed him.

"I would never have hurt Pete," she said softly. "It wasn't me."

His eyes flew open once more. "Yes. It was you. If you hadn't come into his life, my son would still be alive."

Hurt twisted inside her. Maybe he was right. Maybe this was her fault.

"I'm sorry."

He grabbed her by the arm and dragged her toward the kitchen. Heart pounding, she stumbled past where Shane had been stabbed to death.

She understood now. He was going to kill her. Tears welled in her eyes.

He forced her into a narrow hall, past a bathroom and a bedroom, to a room where the hall ended.

He shoved her into the room and turned on the light.

"Look!" he ordered, gesturing to the floor with the weapon.

She stared downward where old, worn carpet—probably original to the decades-old trailer—covered the floor. Shag carpet. The colors were faded, but there was no denying what they were…blue and *green*. Understanding settled in. These were the green and blue fibers found in the bed where she was assaulted and on Pete's shirt.

This was the evidence that had been suppressed…the single piece of evidence that proved someone besides Rory and Pete had been in the cottage that night.

She looked to Anthony. "Then you know."

He nodded. "I've known from the beginning."

Chapter Eighteen

Scottsboro Police Department
South Broad Street
Scottsboro, 9:40 p.m.

Rory was not in the police station. Anywhere.

The parking lot was empty.

Chance's car was still there. He'd had the fob anyway. She couldn't have taken it if she'd wanted to.

Detective Fowler walked toward him. Chance wanted to punch the guy. If he had not insisted on interviewing them separately, this would not have happened.

Fowler explained, "Officer Ridley said Ms. Harris was approached by an older man and shortly after left with him. The video surveillance footage showed she left with Anthony Harris."

"Are there cameras in the parking lot?" Chance asked, worry making his blood pump faster through his veins.

"They turned left out of the parking lot, which doesn't help a lot."

Fury slashed through Chance then. This was way beyond the pale. "You and I both know she did not kill Pete Harris. We also know, based on a meeting with Rick Hill, that he killed Pete Harris and was working with someone he considered untouchable, protected. In other words, a cop."

"You have no proof of any of that," Fowler argued. "You're speculating."

He sounded more like a lawyer than a damned detective. "Trust me, Fowler, unless Hill ends up as dead as Carter, he'll roll over on the guy as soon as he hears he's dead. Whatever happened that night, Carter is going to take the fall for everything. The headlines won't do a lot for your department or the sheriff's department."

"I've already issued a BOLO on Anthony's SUV."

Chance almost laughed. It was about time the guy did something right. "We should go to the Harris home and see if he took her there."

Fowler frowned. He reached into his pocket and withdrew his cell phone. Every instinct Chance had elevated to high alert.

"Detective Fowler," he said, answering the call.

Chance barely restrained the urge to run outside and get in his car and drive. He had to find her. But he had no idea where to start. As much as he despised the idea, he needed Fowler's help.

"I will keep you advised," Fowler was saying. When he ended the call, he looked at Chance. "That was Mrs. Harris. She's concerned because her husband left the house hours ago and has not returned. He was in a rage. She's worried…"

Which meant he wasn't at their house. Damn it. "That he might hurt someone?" Chance demanded.

Fowler let out a big breath. "She has no idea."

Of course she didn't. "We need to go to the cottage," Chance ordered. "He might take her there. Maybe his fear that her conviction will be permanently overturned has him bent on revenge."

"Hold on." Fowler held up a hand as he made another call. He ordered a detail to the cottage and to Rory's house on Tupelo Pike. He put his phone away then. "I think we will be better served to wait until we hear back from the officers I've just sent to the locations of interest in this case."

Except…Chance realized…he'd forgotten one place. "Mr. Harris has stayed in the background since Rory was released. But tonight, after the news about Carter's murder, he's suddenly making a strange and unexpected move."

Fowler frowned. "We should have someone going to Carter's trailer too."

"I'm going." Chance was walking toward the exit before he finished the words.

Fowler hustled to catch up with him. "I'm going with you."

Chance shot him a look but didn't slow. He wasn't sure about this guy. Whether he just failed to do the job or had some reason for suppressing evidence. Either way, Chance didn't trust him completely.

"I'll meet you there," Chance said, not taking the risk.

He burst through the exit and ran to his car. He was out of the parking lot before Fowler had made his way to his own vehicle. He raced across town as fast as he dared. Without Fowler in the car with him, if he was pulled over, he would have a hell of a time convincing the officer to let him go.

He would be lucky if Fowler didn't sic a traffic cop on him. All the more reason to get out of town as quickly as possible.

A margin of relief came when he made the turn onto Old Larkinsville Road. Once he was over the railroad track, he sped up, took the curves as fast as he dared. It took longer than he would have preferred, but soon enough Carter's place came into view. The SUV belonging to Harris was there. Chance wanted to be relieved, but he wouldn't be until he had eyes on Rory and saw she was okay.

He pulled over onto the side of the road, left his car and started for the trailer. He spotted another vehicle parked on the other side of the big black SUV. Smaller SUV. White in color. He looked toward the place where Shane Carter had lived and died.

Someone besides Rory and Anthony Harris was in there.

Carter Residence
Old Larkinsville Road
Scottsboro, 10:30 p.m.

"What are you doing?"

Rory's gaze shot to the door and to the woman who had made the demand. Eudora stood there glaring at her husband.

Anthony looked up at her from the seat he'd taken on the bed. Rory sat next to him. He'd lapsed into sobs, and she had tried to comfort him. The gun lay on the floor at his feet. He'd admitted to killing Shane.

"He knows I didn't kill Pete," Rory explained, some part of her feeling vindicated. "It was Shane."

Eudora's face twisted in equal parts fury and disgust. "What is she talking about?"

The demand was directed at her husband.

"It wasn't her," Anthony said, scrubbing his forearm across his face.

She stormed up to him and slapped him hard across the face. Rory reared back, assuming she would be next.

"We both know it was her," Eudora roared. "Her prints were on the knife."

Anthony dropped his hands into his lap. "Shane wrapped her fingers around the knife."

Eudora's face turned a strange shade of reddish purple. "What are you saying?"

"You were so unhappy. So miserable. I wanted to make you happy again. I wanted to end the turmoil."

"What did you do?" Her words were like a lion roaring at a target.

"They screwed up... Pete wasn't supposed to die," Rory said.

Rory's heart stood still. No...her blood seemed to drain to her feet. *No...this couldn't be.*

Eudora turned to her, and Rory realized she had said the words out loud.

She held Rory's gaze. The shock and realization there made it impossible for Rory to look away.

"No!" Eudora screamed, her attention swinging back to her husband.

Rory stood. She was getting out of here.

Eudora grabbed the gun from the floor and wheeled toward Rory before she could get through the door. "You are not getting away with this. *You* killed my son."

Rory froze, her mind rushing to determine the right thing to do. "No. Shane killed him. Didn't you hear what Anthony said?"

"But it's your fault," Eudora snarled.

The story suddenly unfolded in Rory's mind as if she'd opened a map detailing the events of that night.

"Oh my God. Shane was supposed to kill *me*. Instead he raped me while his psycho friend Rick Hill tortured Pete. But Hill went too far and killed him, didn't he?" Her heart sank at the horrible images playing out in her mind. "Then Shane had to cover it up to protect Pete's father… to protect himself."

"You are insane," Eudora sneered.

Fury rocked through Rory. "No. It was all to protect *you*. You killed him," she accused. "You and your twisted sense of self-righteousness and privilege. I wasn't good enough for you, and your son died because of it."

Eudora leveled her aim on Rory. "I will not let you live when my son lies dead in the cold ground."

Rory dove for the hall.

The weapon fired. The bullet struck its target.

Anthony was shouting. Eudora was screaming.

Rory scrambled forward away from the bedroom door, her skin burning where the bullet grazed her upper arm.

Chance was suddenly there. He pulled her to her feet. "Go. Now. Get in my car and drive away."

She hesitated.

"Go!"

She rushed out the door, blood slipping down her arm. Ran across the yard. Headlights rolled across her, blinding her. The car slammed on its brakes, and someone got out.

"Stop right there!"

Fowler. Rory froze. Her left arm suddenly hurt like hell.

The thudding in her chest threatened to steal her breath completely. She had just escaped a madwoman, and now she was facing the detective who likely helped Pete's parents thwart the law. Dear God, Anthony had done this. How was that possible? What kind of person would go so far to make his wife happy? To stop a marriage?

Rory had signed a prenup. She was no threat to the family's money. She had done everything right. Apparently her only mistake was in loving the son of psychopaths.

"Where's Rader?" Fowler asked, next to her now. He glanced at her arm where the glow from the headlights reflected in the fresh blood.

"He's inside." She turned to the trailer. "Anthony Harris had a gun. He was going to kill me, I think. Then Eudora showed up, and she took it from him. She shot me." She suddenly stared at the leaking wound as if she only just noticed it.

"Get in the car," Fowler ordered, "and stay there. I'm calling backup and going in."

Rory nodded and watched him rush toward the trailer. She put her right hand over the injury and applied pressure. Maybe Fowler was one of the good guys after all. Not the brightest detective, it seemed. But…

But what if he went in there and killed Chance? Then there would be no one to confirm Rory's story. For all she knew, the guy in prison could be dead already.

She rushed toward that porch, practically jumped the steps. At the door she took a breath. Listened.

"You should put the weapon down, Mrs. Harris."

Chance's voice.

Renewed fear surged through Rory's veins. She fought it back and eased through the door.

"Drop the gun, Mrs. Harris," Fowler said. "And let's talk about this."

Rory couldn't see any of them. They were all at the far end of that narrow hall.

She slipped across the living room and into the kitchen.

"Eudora, put the gun down," Anthony pleaded. "We've done too much already. It's time to let it go."

A clunk echoed, and suddenly there was a rush of movement. Eudora was crying. Anthony was trying to soothe her.

Footsteps sounded at the front door. The backup Fowler called had arrived.

Chance suddenly appeared in the kitchen. He was okay. Rory hugged him, the move sending a flash of pain through her arm. Thank God it was over.

The uniformed officers rushed past them. Fowler's voice sounded above the other noise as he read Mr. and Mrs. Harris their rights.

"Let's get you to the ER," Chance said, his arm around her waist and ushering her toward the door.

Rory didn't say a word. She was just glad to be going. Thankful to walk away alive.

And with the truth.

Chapter Nineteen

Friday, July 10

Rental Home
Pine Island Circle
Scottsboro, 10:30 a.m.

Rory walked out onto the deck with her coffee. Thank goodness there was a morning breeze. That Southern summer weather had kicked in full throttle with a healthy surge into the upper nineties.

She sat down, cradled her mug and savored the hot liquid caffeine. It had been just over three weeks since the investigation had burst wide open. Since then, the headlines in every newspaper across the state had heralded her a hero for fighting for the truth. But the truth was, Chance was the hero. The Colby Agency was the hero. She had said as much in the one interview she had granted.

It still stunned her each morning when she woke up and remembered all that had happened since her release from prison. Between Rick Hill and Anthony Harris, they had gotten the full story. All Anthony had wanted was for his wife to be happy. In the final weeks before the wedding, he'd grown more and more desperate. Having had too many drinks at Pete's bachelor party, he'd said as much to Shane. Blabbed on about how he wished Rory would just go away for good. Shane had decided he would take care of the problem and then blackmail the Harris family. After all, Anthony and Eudora had never treated Shane's mother right. It was time to even that score.

Shane and his partner had been playing their sick games for several years. Pick an isolated house without a security system, take what they wanted, have a little fun and get out. They were good at it—rarely made mistakes. The way they treated the victims, particularly the two women at Henagar just showed the sheer depth of their evil.

The hit on Rory and Pete's wedding night was different—it was personal and escalated to a whole new level of depravity. Shane wanted Rory—just once. He'd been lusting after her for months—maybe just to have what belonged to his cousin. Desperate to help his wife, Pete had fought his captor. The struggle left him bleeding out on the floor. Shane and Rick had freaked out and taken off without finishing the job—killing Rory.

A month later, desire for the money overriding any guilt, Shane told Pete's father what he'd done and why he'd done it. Anthony had been devastated. When he'd threatened to go to the police, Shane had warned that he'd only done what Anthony wanted him to do. Unable to bear Eudora learning the truth, Anthony had kept the awful secret. Two years later, when Rory was granted the opportunity for a new trial, the fear and guilt that had been eating away at both men got the better of them.

It was during the sorting of all those awful details that Rory learned Pete was the one to rent all the cottages in that little cove. He'd wanted everything to be perfect for their short honeymoon. She would miss him always, and he would forever own a piece of her heart.

Now, thankfully, the truth had been revealed, and she could go on with her life.

Austin was beside himself with happiness. The two of them had waded through what was left of Lulu's cottage in search of salvageable family treasures. She smiled at the idea that Lulu's little yellow bug was out in the driveway. Rory had decided to use it until she figured out where she was going and what she was doing next.

The best news of all was Chance. They had spent the past few weekends together, getting to know each other better. But they were taking things slowly. No rushing into whatever came next.

As if on cue, the sliding doors opened, and he stepped out onto the deck. "Good morning."

She set her coffee aside and rushed to greet him. They shared a kiss. "Your flight okay?"

"It was."

He'd flown from Chicago to Nashville early that morning and driven down. He would be staying the weekend again. Rory couldn't wait to tell him her news.

"I was thinking," she offered as they stood together, arms around each other and staring out over the water, "that we might have a late breakfast out somewhere." They'd spent most of their time right here hidden away to avoid the reporters. But things had calmed down now. Plus there was a new restaurant in nearby Guntersville that served breakfast all day.

"Sounds good to me." He kissed her forehead. "Things okay here?"

She nodded and turned to face him. "Things are great."

He smiled, his dark eyes crinkling. "Does that mean you've decided what's next?"

"I've thought about that a lot." She sighed, a happy, contented sound. "I think I'll wait a year before going back to teaching only because I need to work out a few other things first."

"You deserve a break," Chance agreed. "No need to rush into anything."

"I don't want to stay here, though." She frowned. "Too many painful memories. Austin plans to stay in Nashville, so there's nothing holding me here."

His smile widened. "You are a free woman, Ms. Aurora Harris."

"Well—" she hesitated "—there is this one thing that has a hold on me."

He dipped his head and brushed his lips against hers. "What's that?"

"It's you." She tilted her head back, stared into his eyes. "I think we need to take that next step. I may not know exactly where I want to live or work, but I know exactly who I want in my life. I'm not waiting another minute on that part."

He nodded. "If you're certain."

"I am certain." She reached down and started to unbutton his shirt. "Maybe we should start right now. Do a little testing to make sure we're a good fit."

He laughed, the deep sound rumbling in his chest, making her tingle with anticipation. "Oh, I'm absolutely certain the fit will be perfect."

"Only one way to find out." She went on tiptoe and kissed him long and deep. He lifted her and carried her inside.

They undressed each other on the way to the bedroom.
Breakfast could wait. The whole world could wait.
But *this*…this could not wait another second.

* * * * *

Look for

The Missing Couple

the next thrilling story in
USA TODAY *bestselling author Debra Webb's*
miniseries Colby Agency: The Next Generation.

Coming next month from Harlequin Intrigue,
available wherever Harlequin books and ebooks
are sold.

Get up to 4 Free Books!

We'll send you 2 free books from each series you try
PLUS a free Mystery Gift.

FREE
Value Over
$25

Both the **Harlequin Intrigue®** and **Harlequin® Romantic Suspense** series feature compelling novels filled with heart-racing action-packed romance that will keep you on the edge of your seat.

YES! Please send me 2 FREE novels from the Harlequin Intrigue or Harlequin Romantic Suspense series and my FREE gift (gift is worth about $10 retail). I may cancel anytime by emailing ReaderServiceInfo@Harlequin.com or by calling 1-800-873-8635.If I don't cancel, I will receive 6 brand-new Harlequin Intrigue Larger-Print books every month and be billed just $7.19 each in the U.S. or $7.99 each in Canada, or 4 brand-new Harlequin Romantic Suspense books every month and be billed just $6.39 each in the U.S. or $7.19 each in Canada, a savings of 20% off the cover price. It's quite a bargain! Shipping and handling is just 75¢ per book in the U.S. and $1.75 per book in Canada.* I understand that accepting the free books and gift places me under no obligation to buy anything—they are mine to keep for free no matter what I decide.

Choose one: ☐ **Harlequin Intrigue Larger-Print** (199/399 BPA G3CD)   ☐ **Harlequin Romantic Suspense** (240/340 BPA G3CD)   ☐ **Or Try Both!** (199/399 & 240/340 BPA G3CE)

Name (please print)

Address   Apt. #

City   State/Province   Zip/Postal Code

Email: Please check this box ☐ if you would like to receive newsletters and promotional emails from Harlequin Enterprises ULC and its affiliates. You can unsubscribe anytime.

Mail to the Harlequin Reader Service:
IN U.S.A.: P.O. Box 1341, Buffalo, NY 14240-8531
IN CANADA: P.O. Box 603, Fort Erie, Ontario L2A 5X3

Want to explore our other series or interested in ebooks? **Visit www.ReaderService.com or call 1-800-873-8635.**

*Terms and prices subject to change without notice. Prices do not include sales taxes, which will be charged (if applicable) based on your state or country of residence. Canadian residents will be charged applicable taxes. Offer not valid in Quebec. This offer is limited to one order per household. Books received may not be as shown. Not valid for current subscribers to the Harlequin Intrigue or Harlequin Romantic Suspense series. All orders subject to approval. Credit or debit balances in a customer's account(s) may be offset by any other outstanding balance owed by or to the customer. Please allow 4 to 6 weeks for delivery. Offer available while quantities last.

Your Privacy — Your information is being collected by Harlequin Enterprises ULC, operating as Harlequin Reader Service. For a complete summary of the information we collect, how we use this information and to whom it is disclosed, please visit our privacy notice located at https://corporate.harlequin.com/privacy-notice. Notice to California Residents—Under California law, you have specific rights to control and access your data. For more information on these rights and how to exercise them, visit https://corporate.harlequin.com/california-privacy. For additional information for residents of other U.S. states that provide their residents with certain rights with respect to personal data, visit https://corporate.harlequin.com/other-state-residents-privacy-rights.

HIHRS2603